My Boyfriend Marks Trees
A MOONSTRUCK MATING
BOOK TWO

EVE LANGLAIS

My Boyfriend Marks Trees © 2024 Eve Langlais

Cover by Atra Luna's Book Cover and Log Art © 2024

Produced in Canada

Published by Eve Langlais

http://www.EveLanglais.com

E-ISBN: 978 177 384 5265

Print ISBN: 978 177 384 5272

ALL RIGHTS RESERVED

This book is a work of fiction and the characters, events and dialogue found within the story are of the author's imagination and are not to be construed as real. Any resemblance to actual events or persons, either living or deceased, is completely coincidental.

No part of this book may be reproduced or shared in any form or by any means, electronic or mechanical, including but not limited to digital copying, AI training, file sharing, audio recording, email and printing without permission in writing from the author.

CHAPTER 1

Skree!

The brown squirrel with a white streak on top of his head—which Ares and his siblings had nicknamed Skippy—had plenty to say about Ares sawing the tree.

So did his wolf.

One bite and it will be quiet.

His reply to his furry other half? *You know how I feel about ingesting raw meat in this form.*

I've seen how you eat your steak.

Difference is steak isn't covered in hair and is delicious.

On that, at least they agreed.

"Sorry, little fellow, but this sucker is slated for the market," Ares told Skippy. The entire field had been originally started by his dad more than two decades ago. When his father passed, Ares took over the planning and maintenance of the fir, spruce, and pine trees that people coveted for the holiday season.

The worst part of the squirrel's harangue? It didn't even have a nest in that particular fir. None in the other three it freaked out about, either. It would seem Skippy had claimed the entire field as his own.

Ares crouched and continued sawing.

Grack. The agitated squirrel yelled before it dumped snow on Ares' exposed neck.

"Bloody hell!" He rolled to his back and gave it a glare. The critter didn't seem impressed, as it continued to harangue him.

Bullied by a rodent. The humiliation, his wolf lamented.

Honestly, more annoying than embarrassing. Ares bared his teeth and growled.

The squirrel proceeded to let loose a stream of pee, and Ares only barely managed to avoid getting drenched.

"Keep it up and I will eat you," Ares warned. The squirrel gave him the critter equivalent of a "fuck you" and leaped to another tree, one better suited for the creature since it hadn't yet reached the proper size for selling and Ares had no plans to take it down yet.

Once more, Ares crouched under the lowest boughs and finished cutting. Then, because there lurked a little boy inside him, he yelled, "Timber!" as it fell onto the frozen ground, puffing the thin layer of snow.

He got caught. His younger sister, Selene—who could sneak like nobody's business—chirped, "For a second, I thought you might start singing that Timber song by Pitbull and Ke$ha."

"Never. You know I don't do that modern-pop shit," he grumbled.

"Or Christmas music or anything with a fun rhythm," his sister complained.

"I like the classics." The classics being Kiss, Led Zeppelin, and AC/DC. He'd grown up listening to it because of his dad and found it more satisfying than anything put out today.

"You're like an old man stuck in a twenty-seven-year-old's body," she said with a shake of her head.

"Not old, more like an enjoyer of the classics."

"No wonder you're still single. Maybe you should try hitting up the retirement homes. I'm sure someone there will appreciate your taste in music."

"Ha. Ha. So funny. What's up? Did you need something?"

"More like wondering if you need a hand at the market?" she asked.

"Depends. Are you going to complain it's cold and wander off buying everything in sight while I do the work?"

Selene's cheek dimpled as she smiled. "Probably. But I wanted to be polite and offer."

"I'll be fine. I'm just about done loading the truck, and the site is already prepped."

"Sounds like Skippy is not happy with you," Selene remarked as the squirrel dangled from a branch and shook a fist while chattering.

"Skippy needs to find another grove of trees to claim."

Selene giggled. "I think it's a game to him. Every year, you two have the same fight."

They did. And every year his wolf wanted to eat Skippy. It should be noted, on the full moon, when he did run on four feet and in fur, his wolf didn't come near Skippy's field, nor did he eat squirrels, although he did like chasing them up trees.

"You and Mom ready for your trip?"

"Yes!" Selene clapped her mittened hands. "The countdown is on. You sure you don't want to join us?"

"Nah, I'm good." Ares had scored a last-minute cruise deal for his mom and sister that he informed them about early since it was their Christmas present.

"But you'll be all alone for the holidays." Selene's perpetual smile drooped.

"Hardly alone. Athena will be around, and I've got an invite to spend Christmas Eve and Day with the Kennedys." Athena's new boyfriend, Derek, came with a set of grandparents that, while slightly crazy—and no he didn't exaggerate, they had a full-on apocalypse-ready bunker and enough ammo to start a war—were actually pretty fun to be around.

Good treats, was his wolf's addition.

"I'm a little jealous. Grams is probably going to

have the best feast." Selene rolled her eyes and smacked her lips. "Those sugar tarts she sent over were divine."

"I wouldn't know. You ate them all."

"You snooze, you lose," she sang.

"You ate all twelve before I even got home from work," he complained.

"Oops. Anyhow, since you don't want my help, I'm going to pop out for a bit. Got a few bunnies to deliver." His sister raised rabbits both for chasing and selling to restaurants. Mom was the honey and pie queen, whereas Ares, who worked as a mechanic, spent his spare time crafting cheese and growing Christmas trees. Only Athena chose a job that didn't involve the farm, working as a lab tech.

With a cheerful wave, Selene skipped off, a happy woman despite the recent trauma of being kidnapped by a mad doctor who wanted to announce to the world the fact they were werewolves—as in, all three siblings changed on the full moon into four-legged furry beasts.

A good thing Selene came out of it unscathed, or Ares would have found a way to kill the doctor a second time. Don't mess with his family.

Ares twined the last tree before loading it with the others. He'd have to hustle. The market would be opening shortly. At least he didn't have too far to go. Arnprior and the church hosting the holiday fair was just a short ride away from the family farm in Calabogie.

The parking area bustled with some vendors setting up outdoors, while others were inside the church with their tables. Ares had a section already roped off, and it didn't take long to throw up his sign, *Christmas Trees for Sale,* with the pricing by height. Then he lay the bound trees against the sawhorses he'd set up the day before. In the past, Ares used to allow people to come and choose their own tree at the farm. However, there'd been too many incidents with idiots who didn't listen to instructions and proved scary with an axe. Much better to provide them ready to go at the market. The quick and easy cash was for spoiling his mother and sisters. A little extra would come in handy as well, given Athena looked to be expecting a child with her firefighter boyfriend. Not that she'd announced it, but Ares smelled the change in her during their last moon run.

As Ares whirled from his leaning stack to grab another tree, he startled at the sight of a little girl eyeballing him, her cheeks rosy and framed by a woolen red hat. Her matching mittens clashed with her light blue snowsuit.

"Hi," chirped the kid.

"Hey."

"Your trees are squished," she observed.

"They'll fluff out nice once we undo the twine."

The child cocked her head. "Mama says real trees are messy."

"Sometimes, but they sure smell good." Good

enough he'd apparently pissed on them when he was little with no regard for the fact they sat in the living room. Drove his mom nuts, whereas dad always laughed and claimed, *"Boy's just marking his territory."*

"Greta, you better not be bugging that man," a woman called out as she bustled over, her bright pink earmuffs holding back her dirty-blonde hair. She had smooth features, pink lips that matched her rosy cheeks, and bright brown eyes. Nice figure, too, the jeans hugging a curvy frame.

Mmm, she smells nice. His wolf approved.

"He has real trees, Mommy." Greta pointed. "They're squishy now, but he says they smell good and get fluffy. Can we have one?"

"We can't get a tree this year, munchkin."

The tyke's lips turned down. "I know. 'Cause we need food and not fri-vol-ussy things."

Ares found himself tightening as the child inadvertently revealed the real reason they didn't have one.

"One day, I'll get you the biggest tree you ever saw," the woman murmured as she crouched by the child.

"Okay." Greta didn't have a tantrum like some kids. She took it like a champ.

Mom leaned close to whisper, "I saw a snowman wandering."

"Snowmen can't walk," snorted the kid.

"Well, this one is, and he has candy canes!"

"Oooh." Greta glanced left and right before spotting the suited character. "I see him!" She bolted for the snowman with candy.

The woman rose. "Sorry if she disturbed you."

"Nah, she was fine. Cute kid."

Fine pup, wolf agreed.

"Precocious with no filter, you mean."

His lips curved. "She is. She mentioned you guys don't have a tree. Why don't you take one, on the house?"

She eyed him, her expression suspicious at the offer. "I don't need your charity."

"Hardly charity. I already know I won't sell all of these. Therefore, you taking one now saves me carting it back to my place."

Her lips pursed. "While your offer is kind, I'm afraid I don't have a way to get it to our place. But thank you."

With that, the pretty woman turned, that sweet ass of hers mesmerizing—*good enough to bite*—and headed after her daughter.

Ares found himself glancing at the woman often as she strolled the Christmas market, not buying anything but managing to give her kid a fun afternoon that included face painting, a visit from Santa, and, of course, a fistful of candy canes. He even spotted her walking away, holding the tyke's hand as they sang carols, not heading for a car but moving out of sight on foot. Probably lived in the area.

When Ares closed up, toting five trees back onto the trailer he'd used to haul them, he noticed a red mitten lying on the ground. A woolen one he recognized with a name stitched inside.

Greta Dawson.

The kid would need it with snow in the forecast and mom tight on dough.

With a tree over his shoulder, and the mitten in hand giving him a scent, he retraced their footsteps. He almost missed the turn onto a side street. His wolf didn't, though.

They went that way.

He pivoted and kept strolling, wondering what he'd say. After all, she'd probably wonder how he found her. He couldn't exactly say he had a super sense of smell. What would sound plausible, instead? It hit him then. He'd seen her filling out a giveaway ballot with the lady who knitted stuffed animals. With the last name on the mitten, he could have easily matched them up.

Excuse found just in time as his wolf huffed, *Here.*

The townhome, which probably had seen better years since it had been built fifty years ago, looked tidy compared to its neighbors. The walkway clear of snow and ice. A wreath, which had obviously been made by a child using colored construction paper, hung on the door. The front window glowed, highlighting the hand-drawn picture of Santa—with a toothy smile a wolf would envy—taped in it.

Ares knocked and stood waiting, slightly nervous. Blame the fact he'd never done anything so bold before, but he couldn't help himself. He could claim he did a good deed returning the mitten, but in truth, he kind of wanted to see the kid's mom again.

When the door flung open, the woman exclaimed, "What are you doing here?"

Ares held up the mitten. "I found this."

Before the woman could reply, there was a blood-curdling scream from inside.

The woman turned and bolted inside the house.

Save the pup!

Ares didn't think. He dumped the tree and followed.

CHAPTER 2

"What is it?" Charlotte yelled as she rushed to find her daughter. Greta stood on a kitchen chair and pointed.

"Ugly bug!"

"Seriously?" huffed Charlotte, only to recoil as she caught sight of it. The bug truly was a hideous thing with many legs and waving antennas. And it moved fast.

"Kill it!" screamed Greta. "It's getting away."

Charlotte hesitated. The idea of squishing it with her sock-covered foot had her cringing.

It scuttled in Charlotte's direction, and she yelped before leaping onto a chair.

The bug knew it had them cornered and stopped between the chairs, wiggling all its nasty body parts.

Stomp. The Christmas tree man, who'd somehow managed to find her, took care of the bug, then apologized. "Sorry for barging in with my boots. I heard the kid freaking and didn't think. Just kind of acted."

Before Charlotte could order him out of her home, Greta literally threw herself at the man, who luckily caught her. Greta wrapped her legs around his torso and hugged him around the neck, crooning, "My hero!"

"Uh..." Tree Man stood there awkwardly, looking unsure of what to do.

"Greta, get down. You can't just maul people. Remember, we talked about personal space," Charlotte chided.

Her daughter leaned her head on his shoulder. "But he saved me and he smells good."

"Greta!" She injected a warning tone.

Did munchkin listen? "He doesn't mind, do you?" Greta turned her gazillion-watt gaze on him, and no surprise, he couldn't escape the cuteness, as evidenced by the smile he returned to her.

"It's fine. I've carried much heavier, and I'm always happy to rescue ladies in need."

"Ladies." Greta giggled. "I'm a little girl."

"Yes, you are. And I think you forgot this." He still held the red mitten, which Charlotte had thought lost since they arrived home with only one.

"Ooh. Thank you." Greta snatched it and waved. "See, Mama, not lost."

She rolled her eyes. "You got lucky. Now say thank

you to the man and goodbye, as I'm sure he's got somewhere else to be."

"Does he have to go?" asked Greta, using her best pleading voice and big, big eyes.

"I wasn't planning on intruding. Just delivering the mitten and one other thing."

"What other thing?" Charlotte asked suspiciously.

"I brought you one of the leftover trees."

Again, Charlotte had no time to reply because Greta squealed. "A tree! A real one! For me?"

"Yes, for you." He laughed. "If you give me a second, I'll bring it in."

"I don't know if you should," Charlotte stiffly replied. "I don't have anything for it." Not a pot, or a stand, or even decorations.

"Don't worry. I've got you covered." He winked at Greta. "You let me know where I'm putting it."

Pretty much anywhere, seeing as how they lacked furniture, the love seat in the living room being the only thing of size. Their small television sat on a battered dresser she'd grabbed from the curb on garbage day. Charlotte kept meaning to paint it.

Greta bounced and clapped in the small entryway. "Oh, Mama. Look. A tree. A real one. It's a Christmas miracle."

While Charlotte hated charity, and the fact this stranger had somehow found them, she wasn't about to crush her daughter's happiness. Time enough to put this man in his place. And if he tried anything... She wore a switchblade on her beltloop for a reason.

A woman couldn't be too careful. Having been a survivor of violence, and hating that helpless feeling, she'd taken self-defense classes. She also went on YouTube and studied how to fight with more than just her fists. Because if *he* ever found her, she needed every advantage she could get.

"Where am I putting it, little princess?" asked the man as he returned with a tree much bigger than the scraggly remnant she'd expected.

"Right there. In front of the window." Greta pointed.

"A most excellent spot. Let me park it here for a second, though, while I grab the stand. I'll be a few minutes. It's in my truck parked at the church."

He must have jogged there and back because it took him less than five minutes to arrive with the stand. It proved to be a metal basin placed within a cube built of two-by-fours.

"How fortuitous you had all those things in your truck," Charlotte drawled, not hiding her suspicion he'd carefully plotted his invasion of her home.

"Some people like the idea of a tree but don't have the stuff to put it up. So I always make sure I've got a few stands and buckets just in case," he tossed over his shoulder as he planted the tree in the contraption. "Fill the basin with water to keep it lasting longer. If it gets dry, the needles will start falling."

"I'll get some water!" Greta ran to the kitchen.

It gave Charlotte a chance to ask questions. "Exactly how did you find us?" Because she was unlisted for a reason.

"Once I found the mitten, Carrie, the lady doing the giveaway for a stuffie, kindly let me sift through the ballots to see if I could match the name. Didn't find a Greta Dawson, but there was a Charlotte Dawson."

A plausible explanation and more trouble than she'd have expected a man to go through just to return a mitten. What did he really want?

Greta returned with a bowl full of water, which slopped despite her careful steps. Charlotte used her socks to mop the spill rather than leave him alone in the room with her daughter.

The tree man helped Greta pour it in. "Okay, stand back now." He pulled a knife, and Charlotte stiffened. The guy grinned at Greta. "Ready for the fluff?"

"Yesss." Greta rocked on her heels with excitement.

The knife slashed the twine, and while it wasn't a window-smashing event like seen in movies, the tree definitely exploded, branches springing out, bulking the tree.

"Oooh." Greta's eyes went wide, and Charlotte wished she could have been the one to bring wonder to her face. They just couldn't afford anything more than rent and food right now. Given she couldn't afford daycare, she could only work while Greta went to school or when the elderly neighbor next door watched Greta in exchange for Charlotte cleaning her house. She'd been scrimping just to make sure she even had a present for Greta on Christmas morning.

When they'd fled, it had been with nothing to their name. Charlotte hadn't dared to hit her place to pack a suitcase of clothes. She'd left her furniture and life behind. Hightailed it clear across the country, from the Rockies to Ontario. She might have gone farther, only she had limited cash left by that point. Only enough to put down a first and last months' rent. Hence why they stayed on the outskirts of Ottawa, in a small town called Arnprior, where a person who wasn't too picky could rent a place that only took two weeks of pay to cover. The other two weeks went to food, which had gotten astronomical in price, plus essentials like clothes for a growing kid and a small emergency fund in case they had to run again.

Greta chatted with the man as he showed her how to fluff the branches. It was when he asked for paper and scissors, which sent Greta scurrying, that Charlotte crossed her arms and said, "What are you doing?"

"Bringing joy?" he offered with a crooked grin.

"Seriously?" She arched a brow. "Exactly what is your game? I have nothing to give you."

"Not asking for anything."

"I'm not putting out either. So if you're expecting any favors because of that"—she pointed to the tree—"then you'll be disappointed."

His lips pursed. "I'm not that kind of man. Listen, I know this might be hard to believe, but I genuinely just wanted to spread some happiness. It's how I was raised." He stood and held out his hand. "It occurs to me that we've never properly met. I'm Ares McMurray, and before you think I'm lying or a serial killer, here's my card." He handed over a black-embossed business card with the title *Ares Artisanal Cheese*, a website address, and a phone number.

"You make cheese?" She couldn't help sounding a little incredulous.

"Yeah. The best you've ever had," he boasted. "But since it's not exactly bringing in the big bucks, I also work at a garage."

"How do I know this is real?"

"Google it. I'm legit. If you want, you can call my mom and sisters too. They'll vouch for me."

Greta returned, waving paper and scissors, the paper technically already used; one side had flyer info on it. Charlotte's work had printed too many for a sale they were having, and rather than dump them in the garbage, she'd brought them home for arts and crafts.

"I gots it!" Greta squealed. "What are you gonna do with it?"

"Well, this tree is kind of naked, little princess. What do you say we give it some snowflakes?"

"Yesss." Greta plopped down and watched as Ares joined her, showing her how to fold the paper accordion-style before trimming bits and pieces and then expanding it with a "Ta-da!"

"Pretty." Greta fluttered it to the tree and draped it. "Let's make another."

"Your turn." He guided Greta without touching, which Charlotte appreciated, and soon her munchkin had her own snowflakes on the tree.

It led to Charlotte murmuring, "I think we have some popcorn we can string too." Might as well join in since the tree was staying.

An hour later and the tree had paper snowflakes, macaroni and popcorn garland, and Greta's prized knock-off Cinderella princess sitting at the very top, courtesy of Ares, who finagled a way for her to stay up there. It was just missing lights, and her work had those for five bucks a strand. She'd just skip buying meat for a few days.

Greta rubbed her tummy. "I'm hungry, Mama."

The late afternoon had turned into dinnertime, and Charlotte gnawed her lower lip because the right thing to do would be to invite Ares to stay for dinner, only the leftover casserole was barely enough for two.

"Why don't you wash up, munchkin, and Mama will fix something."

As Greta skipped out of the room, Charlotte's cheeks heated as she mumbled, "I'm sorry, but I haven't done groceries and—"

"No need to apologize or explain. I know I've

overstayed my welcome, or should I say, barging in? You've got a sweet kid."

"I know."

"Thanks for not poking me with your knife. I know I kind of took you by surprise."

Her eyes widened. So he'd noticed it. "Thank you for not being a psychopath."

His lips curved. "Just a weird dude who sells Christmas trees and makes cheese. I should get going now. Mom's usually got dinner on the table by six-thirty, and it will take at least a half-hour to get home."

"You live with your mom?" It came out a little judgey.

"Me and my baby sister. We don't like Mom being alone, especially since the farm always needs something done. My older sister, Athena, moved out, but she comes by often."

A man close to his family. Sweet and rare these days.

Greta skipped back in and saw Ares putting on his coat. "You're leaving?" Her lips turned down.

"Yeah. But I had a fun time. Thanks for letting me help decorate your tree."

"You're welcome. When are you coming back?"

"I'm not sure, princess. I think that will depend on your mom."

Charlotte hadn't been interested in any man since the sour experience with Greta's dad, so it surprised when she muttered, "Maybe he can come back for dinner another time."

The smile he beamed her way almost impregnated her. Her ovaries certainly did a little jiggle. Jeezus, no way was he single. Or if he was, definitely a player.

"I would love to come back for a visit. 'Til next time, little princess."

Greta threw herself at his legs and squeezed. "Bye, Ares."

Charlotte saw him to the door and murmured, "Have a good evening."

"You too, Charly."

Wait, Charly?

She was still blinking at the nickname as he crossed the street to a pickup truck. Stared at his ass in his snug jeans and wondered why a man like him would even be interested.

At twenty-five, with a six-year-old, and a few pounds too many—*"you fat cunt, you disgust me"*—she had no illusions about how men saw her. Maybe he really just was a nice guy trying to spread joy.

Not that it mattered. She'd most likely never see him again. Still, she didn't toss his card but stuck it to the fridge. After all, she did love cheese.

CHAPTER 3

Ares found himself not caring that his favorite station played Christmas tunes instead of their usual heavy metal. In fact, he even hummed along as he headed home. While he'd only planned to drop off the tree and mitten, he found himself spending two hours with Charlotte and her kid. He'd never seen himself as the domestic type, but there'd been something really nice about hanging with them. Making decorations like he used to when he was a boy. Soaking up the joy oozing from Greta. Finding himself watching and being all too aware of Charlotte, the woman who eyed him with suspicion.

With reason. He could see why she might be leery. His actions weren't just out of character; they could be seen as creepy. He'd almost stumbled giving a plausible explanation for how he'd known her address. Luckily, she had filled out a giveaway ballot so she didn't completely catch him in a lie but it had been close especially since he'd not known her first name when he'd gone knocking. Only by chance did he see a piece of mail lying on the table addressed to Charlotte.

All that trouble to meet her, and he doubted she'd invite him back. The offer for dinner was likely made to placate Greta. Still... she did have his number.

She won't call.

His wolf seemed certain and was probably right, which kind of bummed. He wouldn't have minded getting to know Charly better. Charly... the nickname had slipped from his lips as if it were the most natural thing in the world.

He entered his place to find his mom and sister singing at the top of their lungs to Boney M. To their shock, he joined in with his deep baritone.

It led to them gaping.

"Jeezus, you're like pythons with your unhinged jaws," Ares remarked as he grabbed a carrot from the dish steaming on the stove and popped it into his mouth.

"You're in a good mood," his mother stated as she pulled out some plates.

"Why wouldn't I be?"

"Because you hate dealing with people," Selene remarked.

He did. "I sold most of the trees."

"Not surprising, given how late you stayed," Mom observed as she began ladling potatoes and veggies onto the plates.

"Actually, I stopped by someone's place to donate one of the leftovers and stayed to help them set it up."

"Oh, who?" Selene asked, grabbing cutlery from the drawer.

"You don't know them. I actually just met Charlotte and her kid today. Greta, her daughter, lost a mitten, and I returned it. Since they didn't have a tree, I gave them one."

"Wait, you went to give it back in person?" Selene's eyes rounded.

"Well, yeah. They lived just up the road from the church."

"And you just happened to notice where they went when they left..." Selene snorted. "How good-looking was she?"

"That had nothing to do with it," Ares protested, fighting the heat that wanted to rise in his cheeks.

His wolf chuffed. *She knows you're lying.*

"Sure, it didn't," Selene drawled.

"I think that was a very nice thing for you to do," Mom said as she threw hunks of roast pork onto plates.

"Every kid needs a tree, and I don't get the impression Charlotte's got any cash to spare."

"Do they have decorations?" Mom asked.

"We made some, and Greta had a princess doll for a topper."

"I've got some extra stuff if you think they could use more," Mom offered. "I'll put together a box for you to run over."

He almost kissed his mom for giving him the perfect excuse to visit.

"That would be awesome. I was thinking of grabbing them some outdoor lights. Maybe even taking over Rudolph since we don't put him out." As kids, they'd loved seeing their plastic reindeer with its red nose lighting up the front yard. However, they didn't decorate much anymore, something that might change once Athena popped the baby.

"Oh yes, you should." Mom's expression brightened. "And I'll make a pie. Two pies, apple and sugar. Also be sure to grab a jar of honey."

It occurred to Ares that not only was he planning to return but his family assumed he would. Could they sense his interest?

Selene arched a brow. "Since everyone's donating, does the kid want a rabbit?"

"She'd probably love it, but I don't think Charly has the extra funds to care for it."

"As if I'd give her one without food," Selene scoffed.

"You know what, before I show up with a live animal, let me run it by Charly first."

She'd probably say no. Heck, she'd probably glare

at him when he showed up bearing gifts again. How to explain this wasn't charity but just how his family was?

Dinner talk turned to the upcoming trip. Mom and Selene would be leaving in a few days. Their excited chatter filled his moments of silence when his mind strayed to Charly.

Why couldn't he stop thinking of her?

Because she smells just right.

Which meant what exactly? And why his wolf's interest? It had never cared much before about the other women he dated, except for Alice. With her, his wolf had said right from the beginning: *Trouble.* Ares should have listened, as Alice went full-on psycho after two dates, calling him constantly, freaking if he didn't answer—his explanation of being at work not enough to satisfy. Luckily, she'd latched onto another guy who didn't mind the stalking.

Told you she was bad.

Sometimes he wondered what it would be like to be alone in his head. There'd been a time he'd thought himself crazy for hearing that other voice—after all, his sisters never mentioned their wolves talking—but his dad, before he died, had explained some had a closer bond to their beasts than others. Ares, for example, like his dad, didn't need a full moon to shift. It took barely any kind of effort to flip into fur, unlike Athena, who struggled, and Selene, who needed to be really pissed to do it without moonlight.

Being a lycanthrope made him special, but it also

led to issues, such as trusting people with his secret. Mom knew, of course. As did Derek and Derek's grandparents. Their knowing was kind of hard to avoid, given the whole mad-doctor-kidnapping thing where Ares had to go furry to help save his sisters and mom. However, not everyone would be as accepting as they had been. Ares had to be very careful, not just to protect himself but his family, which meant dating had to be done cautiously. His dad had told him that Aunt Jane—Dad's sister—had to kill her husband when he found out because he thought her a monster and pulled a gun on her. Ares hoped to never be put in that position.

Which led to Ares realizing no matter his attraction to Charlotte, he should probably stay away. She was a nice woman, with a great kid. She deserved better than a man with a furry secret.

A thought that led to a restless night.

The next day was Sunday, and since Ares had no markets to attend for selling cheese or trees, he found himself puttering. He fixed a loose handrail going upstairs. Vacuumed. Changed the furnace filter.

Selene finally looked at him after lunch and said, "Dude, would you just go over and see her already?"

"Who?"

"Do not play dumb. It's obvious you're jonesing to see her."

"Am not."

"Says the guy who can't sit still for two seconds."

He frowned. Last night he'd decided that it was best to stay away, but would it really hurt to drop off some extra decorations? Greta would probably enjoy having the plastic Rudolph currently collecting dust in storage.

"Isn't it too soon for me to just show up again?" He'd never been on more uncertain ground.

"Not if you like her."

He blurted out his dilemma. "That's why I don't think seeing her is a good idea."

"What do you mean?"

"Do I really have to spell it out?" He arched a brow.

"Oh, for goodness sake, I'm not telling you to admit you like peeing on trees, but you can be friends, you know."

"Friends?" Friends could eventually become lovers. Or not. Maybe the strange vibe coursing through his body would fade if they spent time together.

Not likely.

"And by friends, I don't mean banging her," Selene said, as though reading his mind. "She's got a kid, which means you gotta be extra careful. No stringing her and the kid along. If you want this woman, then you'd better be 100 percent sure you're ready."

Was he ready?

No.

Maybe.

How could he tell?

"Maybe I should just forget it," he mumbled.

"What are you afraid of? Falling in love? Happened to Athena and she's never been happier. Are you scared of happiness?"

"You just said to take it slow and be careful."

"I said to be sure before you break that woman's, and her kid's, heart. So, yes, take it slow. Be careful. Not just of them, but yourself. I don't want to see you rocking and crying in a corner. I'd have to take pics and mock you later."

"You really think I should go over."

"Or at least give her a call or a text."

"I don't have her number."

"In that case, visit, but not empty-handed. Have an excuse."

Advice he took and how he ended up on Charlotte's front stoop, carrying a large shopping bag in one hand and balancing a pair of pies in the other.

The look on Charlotte's face went through a few stages; trepidation, surprise, suspicion, and, finally, a rueful shake.

"You're back."

"Yeah. I told my mom and sister about you and Greta and the tree, and well, we had a few things lying around that we don't use that we thought Greta might like. Tinsel and some other decorations."

"Were the pies lying around too?"

"Mom likes to bake. She also sent a jar of her honey. And I brought cheese," he finished, trailing off.

"Why?"

Because she's the one.

A furry claim that startled him so much his dumb ass blurted out, "'Cause I like you."

CHAPTER 4

Charlotte blinked as she processed his words then snorted. "Are you high?"

"Er, what?"

"We met yesterday and hung out for like two hours. Most of which you spent making decorations. Then you show up today, laden with stuff, saying you like me?" Her gaze narrowed. "What are you really after?"

"A chance to get to know you."

She shook her head. "I am not looking to date anyone right now."

"Which I respect. I was just being honest. I'm kind of surprised by it myself."

Her gaze narrowed.

"That didn't come out right. More like, I wasn't looking for a relationship either. Then you and Greta appeared and, well... What can I say? There's something about you that I can't seem to ignore."

"Must be my shining personality," her dry reply. At the same time, what he said struck a chord. Made her feel warm and attractive. It had been a while since that happened.

His lips twitched. "I don't mind a strong, confident woman. After all, I'm the only boy in the family. I am used to being bossed around."

"I highly doubt anyone can make you do anything you don't want."

"You'd be surprised. Selene won the second serving of Mom's shepherd's pie last week. She gives a deadly purple-nurple."

Charlotte blinked. "Your sister attacked you?"

"More like asserted her claim on dinner."

"Sounds like abuse."

He snorted. "Hardly. Abuse involves tears and bruises and fear. When we roughhouse, it always ends in laughter."

"I wouldn't know. Only child."

"Speaking of my sister, she actually told me to take things slow with you. That rather than jump into dating, we should see how we are as friends."

"You talked to your sister about me." Like, holy slam on the brakes. She'd just met the guy, and he was having discussions about a nonexistent relationship. She didn't know if she should be flattered or get a restraining order.

"I also mentioned you and Greta to my mom." He held up the pies. "Which is why she baked these special for you." He lifted his other arm. "And she put together some extra Christmas stuff for Greta."

"What did your sister send?" she asked with an arched brow.

"Nothing. Yet. She did ask if Greta was allowed to have a rabbit. She raises them on the farm."

Charlotte pulled the door shut and hissed, "Don't you dare mention that to Greta. I don't have the money to take care of a pet."

"Selene said you wouldn't have to worry about that 'cause she'd supply everything it needs."

"No. Just no." She shook her head.

"No to what?"

"You. This. Everything. There is something weird about you, Ares McMurray. You are too good-looking to be trying so hard to get in my good graces."

"You think I'm attractive?" He grinned and got even more handsome.

"Don't you play cutesy with me. You know you're hot, and no hot guy is this nice with someone who's been barely polite with him."

"I understand why you're standoffish. You're obviously working hard, with being a single mom and all. I'm a guy, and I know for a fact some of us can be scum. And you've got Greta to watch out for. Can't let just anyone close to that sweet princess."

She stared at him. "Is someone whispering in your ear telling you all the right things to say?"

"No, although my mom's often in my head yattering on about being a gentleman and doing unto others and all that."

"I told you before I don't need charity."

"This isn't charity."

"Then what is it?" She crossed her arms.

"Me putting my foot in my mouth?" He offered a wry grin.

"Ares!" Greta flung open the door and squealed at the sight of him. "You came back."

"I most certainly did, and I brought pie."

"Oooh. What kind?" Greta asked, craning on her tiptoes.

"Apple and sugar."

"I wuv it!" The tyke stretched her fingers as if to grab.

"Not until after dinner!" Charlotte exclaimed.

"Awww." Greta pouted, and Charlotte could see Ares struggling as he got blasted with the cuteness. Before he could cave and hand the kid the pies, she muttered, "Bring it inside."

"Actually, this is just the first load." He handed over the pies to Charlotte and the bag to Greta. "I've got some more stuff in the truck."

Before Charlotte could argue, he returned with another box. Inside was a plastic-covered container and an unopened package of uncooked spaghetti, as well as a shaker of parmesan. "I brought some of my mom's sauce. Thought it would make a tasty dinner."

"Ooh, 'pagettis!" Greta crooned.

"I also brought something very special. Something my dad used to put on our front lawn every year. But now that we're, like, super old, I thought a certain princess could use it instead. How do you feel about having one of Santa's reindeer in your front yard?"

"Is it Rudolph?" Greta asked, wide-eyed.

"How did you guess?" he exclaimed.

"He's my favorite."

"Mine too!"

And that was why and how Charlotte's tiny front yard suddenly ended up with an ugly plastic reindeer and lights that wrapped around her front door and window.

Charlotte wanted to be mad. Instead, she melted like a marshmallow in hot cocoa. How could she not? Ares enlisted Greta's help, letting her climb the ladder he'd brought but sticking close to grab her if she fell. He looked so damned pleased when they plugged the strand in and Rudolph's nose turned pink, the faded red plastic no longer bright.

Greta soaked up the attention, and it gave Charlotte a pang. If only Greta's actual dad had been so nice. But everything changed after her birth.

When they came inside with rosy cheeks, Charlotte murmured, "How old is that thing?"

"My dad bought it when Athena was born, and she's twenty-nine now."

"It's practically a family heirloom," she noted.

"It is, but me, Mom, and my sister agreed it was time it stopped gathering dust and brought joy to another kid."

She shook her head. "You're something else, Ares."

He was also unlike any man she'd ever met. He sang along to cartoon Christmas carols with Greta as they added more decorations to the tree, including a strand of lights he'd brought. A fortuitous thing, since she'd forgotten to grab some.

"Don't you need this stuff for your place?" she'd asked at one point.

"We've got tons more. Mom used to go nuts."

"Used to?"

"She says it's not the same now that we're all grown up. Although that will change next year most likely since my big sister might be preggers."

"You'll make a good uncle," Charlotte stated.

"Yeah, I will." He grinned. "I plan to be the fun one. Gotta make sure my niece or nephew loves me more than Selene."

"You're going to compete with your sister?"

"Heck yeah. It's a sibling thing." He laughed.

Charlotte shook her head. "If you say so. I wouldn't know. Like I said before, only child. By choice. My parents weren't exactly thrilled with the whole child-raising thing."

"Sorry to hear that."

"Meh." She shrugged. "It's how they were."

"Are they at least better grandparents?"

"No, because they died not long after I got pregnant with Greta. Freak animal attack when they were on a nature hike."

"Shit." His mouth rounded. "Sorry, didn't mean to swear in front of Greta." Greta hadn't noticed, as she was coloring in a Santa from the activity book Charlotte splurged on at work.

"She knows not to repeat bad words." Charlotte saved him from his chagrin. Not many guys would have apologized.

"I'll try and watch my tongue. Speaking of tongues, mine's getting hungry. Let me get dinner started."

"I can do it," Charlotte quickly said.

"Nope. I barged in. I will cook. And clean!" he added.

He meant what he said. He got two pots going, one for the sauce, the other for the pasta. Charlotte set the table and toasted some sliced bread, which she buttered and sprinkled with garlic. Not a baguette, but it would sop up the sauce nicely. He'd brought enough to make at least another dinner and maybe even a lunch.

The meal proved discomfiting, as he paid equal attention to her and Greta. Praising her artwork, asking about her kindergarten class. He also inquired as to where Charlotte worked, which led to her having embarrassed red cheeks when she told him, "I'm a clerk at Giant Tiger."

"Love that place," he exclaimed. "Best deals around." He didn't make a comment about her working a low-end job.

"Before we moved, I used to work as a receptionist for a dental office. I've applied to a few places. Problem is, no one can check my references as the place burned down and I don't know where Dr. Jones is working out of now."

Ares appeared pensive. "That's unfortunate."

"It doesn't help I don't have a car to get to most of the dental offices, and I can't get one on my current salary."

"I might be able to give you a hand with that. My mom and sister are going on a two-week cruise. You're more than welcome to borrow Mom's car while she's gone."

"I wasn't looking for a handout," she quickly retorted.

"It's called doing a friend a favor."

"I didn't know we were friends."

"We shared 'pagettis," he declared solemnly. "We are officially friends. And friends can loan each other things."

"You said it's your mom's car," she pointed out.

"It is, but I guarantee she'll be fine with it. It's insured and spends most of its time parked even when she is home. Chances are you can borrow it until you upgrade employment and can afford one of your own."

"She seriously wouldn't mind?" This kind of generosity baffled.

"If Mom were here, she'd have already handed over the keys."

"I..." Charlotte ducked her head and looked at her fingers flexing on the table. "I don't know what to say."

"Most people choose to go with thank you, but I'm also okay with, 'Ares, you're so wonderful,' or 'Why don't I cut you a piece of sugar pie to match your sweetness.'"

She blinked at him and, before she knew it, erupted in laughter. "You're too much. Thank you. For everything."

"Did I hear pie?" Greta came flying from the living room, leaving the Christmas cartoons she'd been watching.

The pie was beyond delicious. The day was the most fun she'd had in ages. Charlotte had not realized how tense and stressed she was until she relaxed.

After Ares helped tuck Greta into bed—reading her a story about a snowman first—he didn't make a move on her but said, "I should head out. I'll be back with the car tomorrow after I finish work, so get your resume ready."

"Will you stay for dinner again? I was going to make homemade mac and cheese with ham."

His lips pulled into a wide grin. "One of my favorites. See you tomorrow, Charly."

He left without trying to kiss her.

Left, but glanced back twice before getting into his truck parked in the driveway out front.

Left, but she kept smiling.

Maybe this time the nice guy wouldn't turn into a monster.

CHAPTER 5

Don't wanna work.

Ares' wolf pouted. Heading into the garage for seven a.m. proved tough since he'd spent the night thinking about Charly. He'd enjoyed himself yesterday. Spending time with her and Greta had been awesome. Now that Charly didn't eye him as a threat, she'd opened up. She had a sharp sense of humor, a husky laugh, and a sexy vibe that had him semi-hard the entire time they hung out. Thank fuck for loose jeans and a long Henley.

She'd not spoken much of her past, briefly mentioning they'd been living there about six months after moving from the west coast. When he'd tried to ask why the relocation, a shadow crossed her face and she'd mumbled, "The cost of living got too high."

Which made sense on the surface until you realized

Ontario had the second-highest cost of living in Canada. A glance around her place showed furniture too used to have been worth moving, and so he could only assume she'd left on the fly. Escaping a situation that led to her feeling like she needed to have a knife on her person. At least, she'd worn one their first encounter. He noticed she'd removed it not long after his arrival the day before. A sign of trust? He could only hope.

What could she have been fleeing? No sign of a ring being recently on her finger, and she'd been emphatic about not wanting to date. Had she been trying to escape Greta's dad? He'd not asked, nor had she volunteered anything about the sperm donor. Given how far she'd moved, it didn't seem like dad was in the picture. Or had she intentionally left him behind?

Work let him bum off early, and he headed over to her place, with Selene, who volunteered to bring Mom's car over. More like she wanted a peek at Charly and Greta.

He parked on the street, while Selene placed Mom's car in the driveway. Selene didn't turn up her nose at the shabby neighborhood but rather said, "Your girlfriend's place is the nicest looking on the block." No need to ask how she guessed with Rudolph out front.

"Be nice," he warned.

"I'm always nice," Selene teased.

"You'd better not have my baby pictures on your phone again."

"Who me?" She batted her lashes and was laughing as Charly opened the door.

Before Charlotte could wonder at the beautiful stranger he'd brought, he did a quick introduction. "Charly, this is my sister, Selene. Selene, Charly."

"Nice to meet you." Selene held out her hand, and with a bemused look, Charly shook it.

"Ares!" The squeal led to Greta shoving past her mother to throw herself at Ares.

He lifted and tossed her into the air, to her squealing delight. He then settled her on his hip as he beamed. "Sis, I'd like to meet, her highness, Princess Greta."

"Hi. Nice to meet royalty." Selene waved.

"I'm not a princess for real, silly," Greta snickered. She cocked her head before saying, "You're the bunny lady."

"I am. Guess Ares told you about it."

He hadn't actually, but she might have overhead him with Charly. "Maybe your mom will let you come visit them sometime. We also have chickens and goats."

"What, no cows for your cheese?" Charlotte inquired.

"Nah. Goat's got a nicer flavor to it, and the lactose in it is easier to digest."

"I like cheese," Greta admitted.

"Me too, princess. Me too."

"Come in." Charly stepped aside. "Would you like some coffee?"

"I can't stay," Selene stated. "I need to go shop for a suitcase since mine decided to croak. Stupid zipper busted."

"Maybe if you packed less clothes..." Ares teased.

"Now them's fighting words," Selene growled, which led to Greta giggling and whispering, "She's funny."

"Glad to see someone appreciates me." Selene flicked her hair.

Greta tucked her head against Ares. "I'm helping Mama make dinner."

"Which is going to be delicious." Over Greta's head, he addressed Charly. "I've got to chauffeur Ms. Packs-too-much to the store before dropping her off at home, but I promise to be here by six at the latest."

"Your sister is welcome to join us."

Before Ares could refuse on her behalf, Selene chirped, "I'd be delighted. Need anything while we're out?"

"We should be good."

"We'll be back in a jiffy then," he murmured to Greta as he pried her from his chest.

Her lower lip jutted.

Charly tucked Greta against her and murmured, "Guess we'd better make sure we prepare the bestest supper while we wait."

"Okay." The pout tugged at his heartstrings.

The pup is sad.

Ares knew better than to counter Charly's parenting, but damn, it wasn't easy. He wanted the little princess smiling.

Selene mocked him as they left. "You are so in trouble."

"Trouble how?" he asked as he headed for a store that sold luggage.

"That little girl adores you."

"Can you blame her? I'm awesome."

"Mom's got eyes for you too."

"Does she really?" The truck swerved as he turned to look at his sister.

"Yes, really."

"She told me she doesn't want to date."

"I get the feeling she might change her mind. The vibe between you two is hard to ignore. Just remember what I said and take it slow."

It might kill him because he wanted nothing more than to kiss Charly—among other things.

Sniff her crotch.

Yeah, that might have to wait even longer.

Should pee on her lawn to warn off others.

Again, not something he should be doing in public. The neighbors would call the cops on him.

Shopping didn't take long. Selene walked into the store and picked the girliest, most flowery suitcase they had. She then insisted on getting a gift for the dinner invite, a bottle of white wine.

When they returned and Selene handed it over, Charly's brows lifted. "That wasn't necessary."

"No, but I insist we drink it."

"I don't have wine glasses." Charly opened a cupboard, showing off mismatched cups.

"In college, I used to drink mine out of a travel mug. It prevented me from spilling it."

Charly's lips curved. "No travel mug but I've got plastic sippy ones."

"Sippy cup, please," Selene exclaimed. She glanced at Greta. "We can be juice buddies."

His sister actually meant it. She clinked her pink cup with its spill-proof lid filled with wine against Greta's, which held apple juice. Ares abstained since he'd be driving, but Charly had a glass with dinner, which turned out to be the best mac and cheese with hunks of ham he'd ever eaten. He made sure to tell her so.

"You're just saying that," Charly huffed as he helped her clear the dishes. They'd sent Selene to watch Christmas cartoons with Greta.

"I will have you know I take my food seriously."

"It's just pasta and cheese."

"Not just any cheese, a blend of three, giving it its creamy texture. A hint of garlic, a touch of chipotle, and then the salty hunks of ham." He kissed the tips of his fingers. "Perfection."

"Mama, I'm on television." Greta's excited yell had Charly dashing in a panic to the living room to see.

She instantly froze as the video on screen showed the market this past weekend. People strolling. The stalls. There he was with his trees. And grinning ear to ear, as a snowman handed her a candy cane, Greta.

"What is this?" whispered Charly.

"YouTube video from the weekend. I cast it from my phone to the television." Selene grinned at Greta. "You're a movie star."

"Anyone can see it?" Charly sounded faint.

"Yeah, but at three hundred views, it ain't going viral. Not yet anyhow, but you never know. Maybe the princess will become famous." Selene nudged Greta, who giggled, but Charly turned pure white.

Ares didn't think; he acted, grabbing her by the hands and leading her outside, where she bent over and breathed.

"What's wrong?" he asked.

"Nothing." The faintest of replies.

"Don't nothing me, Charly. You freaked out seeing Greta on screen."

"I'm sure it will be fine."

It didn't take a genius to fit the pieces of this puzzle. "You're worried someone will see her."

She glanced sideways at him, still bent over, her hair partially hiding her face. "I'm overreacting."

"So I'm right. You are concerned."

She straightened. "Yes, but like your sister said, doubtful it goes viral. I mean, who cares about a small-town Christmas Market?"

"Care to tell me what's got you scared?"

For a second, he didn't think she'd reply. Then she whispered, "He can't find us."

"He who?"

"Greta's father." She turned from him. "I know that sounds horrible, but trust me when I say she's better off far away from him."

"Did he hurt her? You?"

She shook her head. "I'd rather not talk about it. Let's leave it at he's not a nice man. And to give you an example, when Greta was just a baby, he walked out, claiming she wasn't his kid."

"She was, I take it?"

"Yes, and the paternity test proved it," she snorted. "But she was not the right kind of kid, according to him. He called her defective."

"Defective? Is he blind?"

"He never explained. I assumed it was because she was a girl or something stupid."

"What a fucking idiot. Not only is she perfect, Greta's got an awesome personality."

"She is amazing, which is why I had to leave. More than five years after he walked out, he suddenly reappeared in our lives demanding we live with him. When I told him to go away, he threatened to take Greta from me."

"I think a judge might take issue with that."

"Oh, he wouldn't wait for a judge. Barry would

literally snatch her. From the street, school, her bed. He wouldn't care."

"You left to protect Greta."

"I had no choice."

"It's unlikely he'll see the video and figure out you're here."

"You don't know him. He's resourceful." She hugged herself. "Argh. I hate living like this."

"Would it help to know that if he shows, I'll have your back?"

We will eat anyone who tries to harm, agreed wolf.

"No, because I don't want to see you hurt."

"Dear Charly, I'm tougher than I look."

I am. Your skin is too soft.

"You're too darned sweet," she grumbled.

"Nah, that would be the pie."

"It was good pie," she admitted. "There's not much left. I kind of had a piece for both breakfast and lunch."

He laughed. "I swear it's like you're trying to make me fall in love with you."

The words emerged from his mouth, and he froze.

She froze.

They stared at each other.

"Uh…" He had no comeback.

But she did. She leaned up and brushed her lips over his cheek, murmuring, "I'm almost tempted to let you."

Then she went back inside.

And he grinned because she didn't tell him to fuck off.

CHAPTER 6

THE FOLLOWING AFTERNOON, HAVING TAKEN off early from work due to Greta's Christmas concert, Charly, using her new borrowed wheels, dropped off a resume at a new dental office and got an on-the-spot interview. When she met up with Ares outside of Charly's school, she practically exploded upon seeing him.

"I got it," she exclaimed.

"Got what?"

"A new job." Her lips curved. "I start after New Year's."

"That is fantastic!" He lifted her and whirled her around.

She laughed. "Thank you so much. Your help with the ride…" She shook her head. "I don't know how I can repay you."

"You already have by inviting me to a concert. I am stoked."

Her lips pursed. "Says a man who's never been to a school concert before. Let me tell you, it's painful."

"How bad can it be?"

Given Greta was in a split junior/senior kindergarten, it involved some kids crying. One little boy, in absolute hysterics, kept reaching for his mother in the front row. Those not having a meltdown sang off-key while not always using the expected words. There was the kid who picked pompoms off his ugly sweater and threw them. The little girl who yanked another's pigtails. And the finale included a fight over who would ting the triangle because, apparently, the second one went missing.

Despite the drama, Greta was perfect, singing with gusto, wearing a bright red dress Charlotte had picked up second-hand at a garage sale.

Ares beamed like a proud parent when Greta sang her two-line solo and gave her a standing ovation and a whistle at the end, which had her little munchkin beaming so hard Charlotte's heart burst. How could this man who barely knew them act more like a father than Greta's own ever did?

After they returned to her house, in two vehicles since he had his truck, he insisted they go to dinner, his treat. "Your choice," he told Greta.

And of course, her kid, whose idea of fine dining differed from an adult's, hollered, "McDonald's!"

Hence why her first not-at-home dinner date with Ares occurred in a Golden Arches restaurant and not the fun kind she grew up with. It now resembled a black and gray box, but at least the food remained the same. The fries too salty but deliciously crunchy. The Big Mac just as yummy with its sloppy special sauce. Greta had a Happy Meal and was excited about her prize. Ares had a quarter pounder with cheese, a McChicken, nuggets, and an extra-large fry.

"Hungry?" Charlotte teased as he dug in.

"Always. Mickey D's has always been a favorite of mine."

"Me too," chirped Greta.

"Apple or blueberry pie for dessert?" he asked.

"Ice cream," giggled her kid.

A laughter-filled, family moment interrupted by a frisson going down her spine. Her head swiveled, and she scanned the patrons. No one familiar, yet she felt watched, and not nicely. The expression "someone walked across her grave" came to mind.

Ares reached out to grab her hand. "You okay? You look like you saw a ghost."

"Fine. Just being paranoid."

Surely Barry wouldn't have seen the video. Wouldn't have flown so far. Wouldn't be here at this exact location at this exact time.

No way.

She couldn't shake her unease though, and when she pulled the car into her townhouse driveway, she wasn't ready to go inside. She glanced at him. "Do you have to leave?"

"Nope. I'm yours as long as you need me."

She glanced at Greta in her booster seat in the back, which she'd snared from the local church that had resources for single, low-income parents. "Want to go see some Christmas lights?"

"Yesss!"

Ares tapped Charlotte's thigh. "If you'll let me drive, I know a house that has the most epic decorations."

"Be my guest."

She emerged from the car and, as she rounded the bumper to exchange spots, put a hand out to stop him.

"What's up?"

"Thank you." This time she didn't kiss his cheek but planted a soft embrace on his lips.

He sucked in a breath but didn't try and maul her. He murmured, "Good thing it's cold outside 'cause the shower I'm going to be taking later is gonna need to be frigid. Damn, woman."

It gave her a thrill to know he found her so desirable, and it led to her boldly saying, "Or you could spend the night. I don't work until nine."

"Only if you're sure."

She cupped his cheek. "No. But that doesn't seem to change the fact there's something about you I can't resist."

"Feeling's mutual." He dropped a kiss on the tip of

her nose. "Better get in the car before princess gets impatient."

True to his word, he drove them past a house done up *Christmas Vacation* style with lights, RV, everything. They spent over an hour slowly coasting up and down the side streets, oohing and aahing at the shining lights. Holding hands, she should add. The car being an automatic didn't need him shifting, and when he reached, she slid her fingers against his.

It felt warm. Right.

Until that moment, she'd not realized just how much she'd missed that intimacy and connection with another person.

It made her all the happier she'd asked him to sleep over. Although she might try and smuggle him out in the morning without Greta seeing him. She did not want to deal with those questions yet. It was too soon.

As they drove back to her place, with a sleepy kid in the back, they heard sirens.

"Sounds like something's on fire," he remarked.

As they turned onto her street, she gasped. Not her place, but the home next door had smoke seeping from a broken window. A truck with flashing lights was parked out front. A huge hose lay on the ground.

A cop stopped the car, and Ares rolled down the window. "Hey, Officer. Is the fire out?"

"Fire's contained, but the area is off-limits."

"But I live here," exclaimed Charlotte.

The cop glanced behind him then back at them.

"Afraid no one's going to be allowed inside that block of homes until the inspectors deem them safe."

"But..." Overwhelmed, she lost her voice, but Greta didn't. "Where are we going to sleep?"

Trust Ares to have a ready solution. "My house."

CHAPTER 7

Ares managed to convince a cop and then a firefighter—by name-dropping his association with Derek—to let Charly run in to grab a few things for her and Greta. Poor Rudolph lay on his side in the front yard and, given the big dent in its ribs from being stepped on, might never be the same.

An ashen Charly emerged from the townhouse with two bulging bags.

Greta in the back seat asked softly, "Are we moving again?"

"More like going on a holiday at my house for a few days."

"But it's almost Christmas. How will Santa find me?"

He paused as he waited for inspiration.

His wolf had it. *Tell her Santa is like a wolf. He can sniff out little kids who've been good.*

Ares modified the advice. "Santa knows all. I wouldn't worry. He'll find you just fine."

He stepped out of the car and popped the trunk for Charly.

She huffed as she heaved her haul into the space and slammed it shut. Only then did she eye him. "Are you sure we won't be intruding?"

"If you ask me again, I am going to kiss you until you can't talk."

She blinked. "That's not really a great threat."

"Then go ahead and ask me."

Her lips pursed. "Not the time."

"Agreed. Now, can you drive? If you can't, then I'll leave my truck here and figure out a ride to work in the morning."

"I can drive."

"You sure? Because it's not a big deal if you can't. I know this came as a shock."

"Wasn't my place that burned." Her lips twisted. "Which is awful to even say. Especially since I know the lady who owns that house. Thankfully she wasn't home when it happened. She is—was—my babysitter. I'm going to have to call in sick to work tomorrow until I can find a new one. Which, again, sounds selfish."

"No, it's you being a mom. And don't worry about Greta. I'll just start my holidays a day early."

No alarm. His wolf liked that bit.

"You shouldn't be so quick to volunteer. It's one

thing to spend a few hours with me around and her toys. But you're talking an entire day with a kid who will get bored of television."

"I live on a farm, remember? More than enough stuff to keep us busy. And I won't be alone. Mom and Selene don't leave until late afternoon." Maybe. The forecast was calling for snow.

"We shouldn't have to impose for long. While the place smells smoky, there doesn't seem to be damage. The fireman seems to think we'll be cleared to move back in within a few days."

"Don't be in a rush." He meant it. He had a feeling once he got used to having them around, he wouldn't want them to leave.

"I hate intruding."

"The house has tons of room. The biggest issue is going to be Mom and Selene."

"Oh dear, will they be upset?"

"Only because their flight is tomorrow, meaning they won't have much time with Greta." He winked.

Charlotte smacked him in the arm. "You're a brat."

"I know. Shall we?"

Ares watched as she climbed into the driver seat and, before the door shut, heard Greta chirp, "Old Mac Ares had a farm..."

Damn, he wished he could be singing along with them.

Instead, he had to drive his truck, keeping his speed sedate, watching in his rearview to make sure he didn't lose Charlotte. They headed out of Arnprior into a more remote area. Calabogie, also known as cottage country, catered a lot to seasonal tourists offering summers by the lake or skiing in the winter for those who wanted a break from the city.

As he drove, he gave his mom a shout.

"Hey, sweetheart. How was the concert?"

"Awesome, but there was an issue after. Just a warning. I'm bringing Charly and Greta to stay for a few days."

"Is everything okay?" His mom's tone held concern.

"Neighbor's place caught on fire, and everyone's been kicked out of their place until they give the all clear."

"Oh dear. How awful. You tell them they are welcome to stay as long as they need. Should Selene and I postpone our trip?"

"Don't you dare! The tickets are nonrefundable. I'll be fine." That, and he wouldn't mind some alone time with Charly.

"I know you will be, but I'm excited to meet your ladyfriend and her daughter."

"You don't have to leave for the airport until early afternoon. Plenty of time to bake cookies with Greta." Because he knew his mom.

"Are they hungry? I'll whip up something for when you arrive. Should I give Greta the daisy room or the honeybee one?" Mom had a theme going in the two guest bedrooms. The five-bedroom farmhouse was made for large families.

"Honeybee has the queen-sized bed, which might be better. I imagine she'll want to sleep with Charly since it's a new place."

"Oh, Charly's not bunking with you?" Mom's less-than-innocent query.

"Mom!"

"What? You obviously like her."

"I am not discussing this with you."

"Such a prude." His mom laughed. "I'll see you shortly. I've got stuff to do."

And by stuff, she meant hanging more than a wreath outside their front door. He arrived to see the bay window lit up with lights and, on the sill inside, her collection of ugly nutcrackers. Her most prized ones. She had too many to sit them all on the ledge—blame him and his sisters. They spent a few years trying to out-ugly the other by hunting for the most ridiculous nutcrackers they could find. The mermaid one with a Santa hat. The pirate with the peg leg. Tropical Santa. At last count, Mom had over thirty of them.

He pulled in first and hopped out as Charly parked behind him. A wide-eyed Greta emerged and exclaimed, "It's a real farm."

"It is." He pointed. "There's the barn where we keep the goats in the winter. And that there beside it is the chicken coop."

"Real chickens?" Greta squeaked.

"Yup. We'll visit them tomorrow and see if they have any fresh eggs for us."

Greta clapped her hands. "Yay!"

"We might even get a chance to milk a goat."

"Cows give milk, not goats, silly," Greta scoffed.

"Greta!" Charly exclaimed.

Ares laughed. "Lots of people think that. If we get enough, I'll show you how I prepare it to make cheese."

"Mmm. Cheese." Greta rubbed her tummy.

Ares grabbed their bag from the trunk and motioned to the house. "Get ready for a warm welcome. Mom is over the moon you're coming to stay. She was even ready to cancel her cruise with Selene."

"Oh, don't let her do that."

"I won't." He chuckled. "Told you she'd be fine with you guys staying."

As they entered, he smelled cookies baking, heard soft Christmas music playing, and saw Selene pop out of the living room with a cheerful, "Welcome!"

"Thank you for letting us stay. We'll try to not intrude." Charlotte had that tense look about her again, and Ares slid his arm around her shoulders for a squeeze.

"Not intruding. Adding joy," he stated.

The usually precocious Greta tucked against his legs and looked wide-eyed at the biggest nutcracker

Mom owned. A hockey player that always had the prime spot in the front hall.

"That's a big nutcracker," Greta whispered.

"Say hello to Jean Guy. Mom's first nutcracker. Dad found it for her."

"He's missing a tooth." Greta pointed to the black spot in Jean Guy's grin.

"Just like the real thing," Ares noted.

"Wait until you see the other ones," Selene exclaimed. "I bought the ugliest nutcracker of the bunch. Come see." She held out her hand, and Greta gripped it, skipping into the living room for a peek.

"Ugliest, and yet she sounds proud," Charlotte murmured.

"Remember that sibling rivalry we spoke of? Poke your head into the living room."

Charlotte did and turned on him with a rounded mouth. "You guys bought those... those..."

"Hideous nutcrackers. Hell yeah, we did." He grinned. "I'm especially proud of the lumberjack, since he looks like dad."

"Your dad was hideous?"

He chuckled. "No, but the wooden version of him is pretty funny-looking. Come on. Let's go find my mom."

Mom wiped her hands on a towel as they entered the kitchen and beamed. "Hello! You must be Charlotte. I'm Beatrice, but you should call me Bea."

"Nice to meet you. Thank you for your hospitality."

"Oh goodness, it's no problem at all. Delighted we can help. Cookie?" Mom, who'd not only managed the quickest Christmas decorating of all time, had also baked. She held out a freshly made, still-hot-from-the-oven chocolate chip cookie.

Charlotte took it and had a bite. Groaned. "Good grief that's good."

"The best," Ares agreed, grabbing three and shoving a full one into his mouth. "Mom's a great cook."

"Where's the princess? I can't wait to meet her." Mom stacked some cookies on a plate and poured a glass of milk before hurrying to the living room.

Charly glanced at him. "You weren't kidding about them being happy about us staying over."

"Mom loves kids. She'd have had more than us three if her uterus would have cooperated. She had to get it removed after Selene due to complications."

"Oh, that must have been difficult for her." Charly nodded sympathetically as she nibbled on another bite of cookie. "I can understand wanting more. Kids are great. Greta was a surprise. I was in college at the time, and things were hard, but I managed. And she's so worth it."

He didn't comment on the fact that some might think things were still hard for her. "You said her father left?"

"Yeah. It was only recently he decided he wanted Greta."

He held her hands and murmured, "You're safe here with me. I won't let anyone take her away from you."

Her lips twisted. "I wish I could believe that. But you don't know him..." She paused. "Barry's a got a dark side to him."

"So do I when my family is threatened." It had emerged recently when his sisters and Mom were kidnapped. To this day, he didn't regret the deaths he'd caused when he'd gone to get them back.

Victory, huffed his wolf.

A victory earned with blood and violence. Had he just been a regular man it might have bothered him more, but half of him was a natural-born predator who saw the world more black and white.

"We should go rescue your mom and sister from my hyper kid," she joked.

Actually, it was debatable who had more energy. They entered the living room to find the three playing Ring Around the Rosie with much laughter when they fell down.

A grinning Greta chirped, "Mama! Ares! Come play."

They danced and sang and ate cookies for a bit before a wide yawn had Charlotte declaring, "Bedtime for little princesses."

"But Mama..."

"The sooner to bed, the sooner you and I can bake some sugar cookies," Ares' mom declared. "After the pancake breakfast, of course."

"Ooh."

"And don't forget we'll be visiting the bunnies," Selene stated, not to be outdone.

"Bah, everyone knows the goats are more awesome," Ares interjected.

Greta beamed and, to his shock, held her arms out to him as she commanded, "Carry me."

For the second night in a row, Ares read a bedtime story while the three of them snuggled—him on one side of the bed, Charly on the other, with Greta in between.

When Greta's eyes drooped, Charly eyed him over her kid's head with matching sleepy eyes. "Not the evening we had planned," she softly murmured.

"Shit happens. We've got plenty of evenings ahead of us." He'd make sure of it. "Why don't you get some sleep, and I'll see you in the morning?"

"Thank you, Ares."

"Bah. It's nothing." He wished he could do more.

He headed downstairs to find Mom and Selene waiting for him.

"She go down okay?" his mom asked.

"Yup. Out like a light. Charly too."

Selene was the one to glance at the ceiling before asking, "What are you going to do if they can't get back into their house by Christmas Day?" Which also happened to be the next full moon when their change into a wolf would be unavoidable.

Whenever possible, he and his sisters ran through the woods in their wolf forms under the full moon. Although, on a few occasions, when they thought they might be watched, they'd spent the night in the windowless storage room in the basement. Not exactly something he could do with Charly in the house. At the same time, him leaving for the night would look suspicious.

"I don't know. I'll figure something out if it comes to that." He raked fingers through his hair. "Hadn't really thought of it."

Selene would be on board the cruise ship when the full moon hit and would spend the evening in their room. Hopefully the staff wouldn't wonder at the wolf hair she'd shed.

Mom had a suggestion. "You could always invent an emergency. Say coyotes are threatening the livestock. Gives you an excuse to be outside and them in here."

"That's not a bad idea, actually." Much as he hated lying to Charly, they were too new in their courtship for him to reveal his hairy secret.

He spent the night tossing and turning, taunted by the fact Charly slept just across the hall.

Let me out, and I'll go watch over them, his wolf offered.

Because waking up to a giant beast won't scare them.

The pup won't be afraid.

Greta might be enthralled with an oversized dog—*Insulting!*—however he couldn't predict how Charly would react. Especially since the dog would disappear as suddenly as it appeared.

Since he wanted to hear them the moment they woke, he left his bedroom door ajar and fell asleep. He woke suddenly, prickling with a sense of being watched, and yet his wolf didn't react.

He opened his eyes to see Greta standing by his bed, staring at him.

She grinned. "You're awake."

"And so are you."

"Mom's still sleeping. She snores," Greta informed him. "So do you."

His lips tilted. "Like a wolf?"

"Wolves don't snore. You're like a bear." Greta giggled.

"A bear who likes honey. And I know where we can find some, along with some pancakes."

Eating made-from-scratch chocolate chip pancakes and chewing on bacon while drinking orange juice was how Charly found them when she entered the kitchen looking a bit frantic. She calmed at the sight of Greta.

"Munchkin, you should have woken me. Sorry if she—"

Mom shook her flipper. "Don't you dare apologize for getting some rest. We're early risers, and she was no trouble at all. As a matter of fact, princess helped make breakfast."

"I got eggs with Ares!" Greta announced. "He has lots of chickens. And after we eat, I'm gonna see bunnies and goats. You coming, Mama?"

Charly shook her head. "I have to go to work. Remember we talked about you being a good girl for Ares while I'm gone?"

"I will be the bestest princess," Greta declared.

It was Charly who struggled. She didn't want to leave, and Ares even told her, "Call in sick."

"I can't. I need this paycheck." Charly's lips turned down.

"We'll be fine," he reassured. "I can text you picture updates if it makes you feel better."

Her lips curved. "I'd like that."

"See you at dinner." He drew her close enough for a soft kiss. "It will be just the three of us since my mom and sister will be leaving for the airport this afternoon. I am going to make my famous fajitas."

"Can't wait."

She thanked his mother and sister for their hospitality and wished them well on their travels. With that, she left, and Ares let Selene and his mom take turns with Greta until they had to get ready to go.

He and Greta waved as they left, and it was finally time for the goats, which were a huge hit, especially the little ones when he dressed them in pajamas.

When dinner rolled around, Charly returned to

find Christmas music, the smell of food sizzling, and an exuberant greeting from Ares and Greta.

What followed was the most domestic evening ever. Dinner, followed by a Christmas movie, story time, and when Greta closed her eyes...

Charly glanced shyly at him and said, "I'm not tired yet."

Hell yeah.

Cuddle time.

CHAPTER 8

CHARLOTTE SPENT THE DAY IN A STATE OF fugue. Not because she'd not slept well—she'd surprisingly fallen off quickly and deeply. The comfortable bed was only part of the reason. The bigger part? Ares, who had a way of making her feel protected and important. Add in the acceptance by his family and her sense of security only increased.

Seeing Greta in her glory—being the center of attention and basking in the happy vibe emitted by everyone—also helped. It had always bothered Charlotte to see the close bonds other kids got to enjoy: the pictures of family dinners and holidays, the grandparents who spent time with the young ones, building memories. Poor Greta had no one but Charlotte. No grandparents to spoil her, nor aunts or uncles, which meant no cousins, either. Barry might have been able to give her some extended family, only he chose abandonment. She'd always found his actions odd considering he was a man who boasted about how close he was to his brothers, not all of them blood.

Then again, knowing what she did now, it was probably for the best Greta never got to know that violent crew.

Ares couldn't have been more different. Self-assured without crossing into arrogant. Generous, giving of himself and expecting nothing in return. Genuinely good-natured. Close to his mom and sisters. Honest in how he felt.

All things that made him sound weak, and yet, he oozed strength, and when he strutted, she practically needed a fan to cool down.

As if he weren't already too good to be true, he and Greta had formed a bond. From the moment he'd killed that bug in her kitchen, her daughter had chosen him to be her hero, and he had yet to disappoint. He didn't ignore Greta when she spoke. He didn't roll his eyes when she wanted to re-read a story or sang the same song a dozen times in a row. He showed patience, explained things to her. Essentially acted like a dad.

Seeing them together, Charlotte melted. This was the family life she'd always wanted, so why did it terrify her?

Because the last time she thought she'd found "the one," he turned out to be a stranger. The act he'd won her over with, just that: a charade. The real Barry turned out to be an asshole. After Greta's birth, the change had been most startling, from loving partner to verbally abusive and rude. *"Jeezus, cover up. I can't believe how much you let yourself go."* She was two weeks postpartum at the time. Months later, she still carried a few pounds, and when she tried to initiate intimacy, he'd recoiled with disgust. *"You can't seriously expect me to get it up with you looking like that."* Still, she'd stayed, hoping for the man she'd fallen in love with to return.

She waited in vain for things to get better, but they got worse. He started going out every night after work. When she'd dared to question his frequent outings, he barked, *"I'll be back when I feel like it. Don't like it? Too bad."*

But the worst had been his accusations. *"Whose kid is she?"*

Her reply of *"Yours,"* led to, *"Like fuck she is. Did you really think I wouldn't find out?"* It didn't matter what Charlotte said.

"I swear, she's yours. You're the only man I've been with."

"Lying whore," was only one of the nasty names he used.

She'd literally only ever been with two men in her life. One in high school and Barry in college. Barry had mentally beaten her down, destroyed her confidence, and made her so suspicious of men she'd chosen to not date. *Am I too fat? Am I that unattractive?*

Logically, she knew Barry was being a dick. Men

flirted with her, and while about thirty pounds heavier than in college, she thought she wore the weight well, her figure curvy in the right places. But a part of her had still heard the burning insults... until she met Ares.

He eyed her as if she were a delicious dessert he wanted to eat. He flirted. He came straight out and said he liked her. Kissed her and made sexy little growly sounds.

Before the fire that rendered her temporarily homeless, she'd been ready to throw caution to the wind and finally make herself vulnerable with a man. AKA, get naked. She trusted Ares to not be repugned. Trusted him to bring her pleasure, not pain. And while their plans the previous evening had been curtailed, tonight, once Greta went to bed, it would be just them in the house.

Just her, him, a bed, and six years of repressed desire.

She hoped she didn't embarrass herself by either freezing up or coming too fast. Was there even a term for a woman who orgasmed prematurely? It might happen. When he kissed her before she left for work, the pleasure had her tightening so hard she'd almost climaxed in the driveway.

Pathetic. *I'm pathetic.* Sigh. And the day dragged. The only highlight—and torture—the regular updates from Ares. True to his word, he documented Greta's adventure at the farm. Greta's open-mouthed laughter as she fed rabbits of all sizes. The look of pure joy as she sat in a barn surrounded by goats—in pajamas! A sight that kind of made Charlotte jealous. She wouldn't mind petting a baby goat too. The baking she'd done with Bea, the pair of them in matching aprons. The picture of Greta walking hand-in-hand with Selene in the woods. Someone even captured a great shot of Ares holding Greta up in the air so she could snag a leaf that remained stubbornly stuck to a branch.

She wished she'd listened to Ares and called in sick.

The day couldn't end soon enough. December twenty-second meant all kinds of last-minute shoppers, and the next few days would be even worse. Then she'd finally get one day off for Christmas before the Boxing Day madness began. Ugh. She really hoped the new job at the dental office worked out because if it did, then next year she'd actually get the week off between Christmas and New Year.

Finally, her shift ended, and she couldn't escape fast enough. The drive to the farm proved simple enough, highway to country road to another country road. She parked behind Ares' truck and noted the Jeep Selene drove was gone. They'd left for their cruise as planned.

Before Charlotte had her foot on the first porch step, the door opened, spilling warm light and delicious smells, as well as an excited kid.

"Mama, you're home!" Greta held out her arms, and Charlotte scooped up her daughter for a hug.

"Hey, munchkin. How was your day?"

"Awesome." Greta proceeded to chatter about it.

Charlotte did her best to reply and pay attention, but her gaze kept straying to the sexy man leaning against the doorjamb wearing worn jeans that hugged his thighs and a plaid shirt stretched across that wide chest. Even his bare feet were sexy. To make things even worse, he gave her the most seductive, panty-wetting smile.

Ares winked and mouthed, "Welcome home."

For the first time ever, it sure felt like it.

"Come inside, Mama. Dinner's almost ready. I helped Ares make it." Greta tugged her by the hand.

As she entered, she peeled off her coat, and Ares hung it and her bag on the hooks in the front hall. He then pointed to some knitted slipper socks as she kicked off her boots. "Mom left those for you. There's also a hat, scarf, and mitten set."

"She didn't have to buy me things."

"Actually, she made them. She sells knitted goods, along with honey and pies in her store."

"When you speak to her, please say thank you."

"Look what Selene gave me from when she was little." Greta dragged her into the living room, where a miniature crib sat beside a wooden highchair holding a plastic doll. "Her name is Pansy."

"She's very cute."

"Of course, she is. She's my baby," Greta said with a sober nod.

"Hungry?" Ares asked.

Yup, but not only for food.

Greta skipped ahead into the kitchen hollering, "I'm gonna get the cheese from the fridge."

Before Ares could follow, Charlotte grabbed his hand and held him back.

He eyed her. "You okay? You seem a little stunned. I know we might have gone a bit overboard."

"You did, but not in a bad way. Thank you. I've never seen her so happy."

"I don't think that kid is ever sad."

"She's pretty good-natured, but this…" Charlotte waved a hand. "When we did the big move, we had to leave most of her toys behind, and while I'd planned to replace them, the money just hasn't been there."

"More important than things, she had you," his soft murmur. "I should be so lucky."

She stepped closer. "Why, Ares McMurray, are you trying to say you want me?"

He uttered a low rumbly sound. "More than you could imagine."

She tilted her chin to look him in the eye. "And what would you do if you had me?"

His arms went around her and tucked her close to his body as he growled, "Make you the happiest woman alive."

He then kissed her, a press of lips that stole her breath—and heart. A kiss that ended too soon as he whispered, "While I'd love to take you upstairs right now, I get the feeling Greta might interrupt."

"I'm surprised she hasn't—"

Right on cue... "Are you guys coming? I'm hungry."

He chuckled. "Finish this later?"

"Yesss." Her turn to be over emphatic.

Dinner tasted delicious and was full of smiles and laughter as she heard about their day.

While she wanted to rush Greta to bed, she controlled herself. She was a mother first. Her daughter deserved more than to be put down early so Charlotte could get some nookie.

When the time came, Ares carried Greta to bed, but they both read the story, taking turns doing the voices of the prince and princess.

When Greta's eyes closed after a mumbled, "Love you," Charlotte's gaze met Ares'.

"I'm not tired yet," she said.

He held out his hand.

Charlotte had never been so nervous in her life. She linked her fingers with his, but rather than lead her into his room, he drew her close in the hallway and began swaying slowly in time to the Christmas music they could hear from downstairs.

Unexpected, but it relaxed her. She leaned her head against his chest and closed her eyes as she listened to the steady beat of his heart. His hands cupped the indent of her waist, and his mouth brushed against her hair.

Soft. Sensual. Also arousing.

She tilted her head and found him staring at her, a slight smile on his lips.

"Hey, gorgeous," he murmured.

Rather than reply, she lifted on tiptoe for a kiss.

It started out slow, a rub of their mouths, an exploration that mixed warm breaths. His hands dropped to palm her ass, and she moaned at the feel of him pressed firmly against her.

She dared to slide her tongue against his, a teasing touch that deepened the embrace and drew that sexy little growl of his.

"It's like you want me to lose control," he murmured, not once letting his lips leave hers.

"Would that be so bad?" To her, the idea he could be so impassioned only made her desire him more.

"How did I get so lucky?" his reply before he drew a startled cry from her as he swept her into his arms.

She wanted to protest—*I'm too heavy; you'll hurt yourself*—but held her tongue because he carried her with ease into his room.

Rather than set her promptly on her feet, he let go of her legs and kept her tight to him, tight enough she could feel his erection pressing against her belly.

Oh my. He appeared to have some size to him.

She stroked her hands over his shoulders and down his thick biceps. Such nice muscles.

"May I undress you?"

His request, so polite, had her nodding, and she shivered as his fingers grabbed the hem of her sweater and lifted it. He removed it, leaving her clad in only her bra, but she didn't feel a need to cover herself with her hands. Why would she when his gaze smoldered?

"Your turn." She tugged his T-shirt out of his jeans, and he helped her to strip it, revealing his smooth, toned flesh. She couldn't resist placing a kiss on his pec, and he groaned.

"You're just determined to make it hard for me to take it slow."

"Maybe I don't want slow," she quipped as she raked her nails down his chest and over his abs.

"My sweet and sexy Charly," he murmured before kissing her again. A short kiss, as he let his mouth trail kisses along her jawline. Nibbled his way down her neck. A good thing he held her because her knees went weak.

He walked her backwards until her legs hit the bed and she sat down. He knelt in front of her, his hands working the button to her slacks. She leaned back to help him tug them off. She kind of wished she wore nicer panties, the pair she had on simple pink cotton.

He didn't seem to care. "You're so fucking beautiful."

No, he was the god in this scenario. His body a work of art. She reached for his belt buckle and undid the loop, then the button fly. His erection bulged against the front of his navy-blue briefs.

Soon he stood there only in his underclothes, his penis technically hidden but also clearly outlined.

He nudged her knees with his muscled leg. They parted, and as he knelt between them, she lay back on the bed. He didn't cover her immediately. He leaned down and pressed his mouth to her thigh. Left, then right. Again, only higher, an anticipatory touch that had her shivering.

His lips teased the inner flesh of her legs, so close to the part of her that quivered with need.

When he pressed his mouth against the cotton gusset of her panties, she arched and uttered a cry, which immediately had her shoving a fist into her mouth lest she wake Greta.

He nuzzled her, teased her through the fabric until she whimpered. Only then did he tug the panties with his teeth, removing them and thus baring her to his view.

But not for long, as he returned with his mouth to kiss her in that most intimate of places. His tongue teased apart her nether lips and lapped.

She clutched at his comforter and gasped and writhed and squirmed. Masturbating just didn't give the same level of pleasure as another person's touch. And it had been so long.

When he flicked her clit, she clenched and came, a small orgasm that left her shuddering.

And embarrassed.

But he chuckled. "There's number one out of the way."

Wait, one?

He wasn't done with her. He kept teasing her pussy, flicking her clit, sucking it, teasing the opening to her sex until she felt her pleasure tightening again.

Again?

She'd not even thought that possible.

When he stopped and moved off the bed, she uttered a soft sound of dismay, but he rumbled, "Just getting a rubber."

The wrapper crinkled as he tore it open, and she rose enough to snag it from his grasp. She was the one to tug down his briefs. His cock sprang forward, eager to meet her.

She grabbed it, and Ares threw his head back and grunted. "Don't play with it too much. I don't know how long I can hold on."

Sexiest thing a man ever said to her. She rolled the condom onto his thick shaft, taking her time stretching the latex over it, squeezing it and enjoying his hissing reaction and the jerk of his hips.

She lay back down and beckoned. "Come here."

"With pleasure," he murmured, covering her body with his own but not crushing her with his full weight. He braced his arms on either side as he leaned in for a kiss. An embrace of such pure sensuality she clenched and writhed under him. The tip of him nudged her sex, and she arched to welcome him inside. He slid in slowly, stretching her, filling her. Torturous pleasure.

When he was fully seated, she couldn't help but

tighten her muscles around him, feeling his shaft pulsing.

A glance at him showed his expression intent, taut, strained, as if he held back.

She reached for him and drew him down for a kiss, and he sighed as he began to pump, a slow rhythm to start. Seesawing in and out. Rubbing her just right. The deep part of his thrust touching a spot that had her gasping.

He kept stroking, his pace getting faster, and she grabbed at his back, dug her nails in, and urged him on. Urged him to thrust harder, quicker. Her pleasure built for a second time, tightened until she exploded, her cry of climax caught by his lips. She shuddered as she came and kept coming, the orgasm that wouldn't end and left her limp.

Only then did he hold himself deep inside, uttering a grunt as he came before he collapsed atop her, breathing hard.

He didn't stay atop for long. He rolled and took her with him so she lay nestled on his chest. "Wow."

"Very wow," she agreed.

His hand lazily stroked up and down her bare back. "I knew it would be good… but damn."

She giggled. "That was insane." She lifted her head to eye him. "Will it always be that incredible?"

His lips curved. "I think it will only get better."

He was right. Their second round, which involved a lot more body exploration, proved just as intense.

Afterwards, they cuddled. She didn't want to leave the warmth of his embrace, even as she fully meant to go to bed so Greta wouldn't wake alone.

Instead, she opened her eyes the next morning to see Greta beside Ares' bed, grinning ear to ear. "Is Ares now my daddy?"

CHAPTER 9

WHILE ARES WANTED TO SHOUT, "*HELL YEAH I'll be your dad,*" he knew it wasn't his place to say such a thing.

Poor Charly looked as if she'd expire of embarrassment. Her face turned beet red as she stammered, "Uh, that is, um, no, Ares is not your dad."

"But you're in the same bed just like a mommy and daddy," Greta explained.

"We had a sleepover," Charlotte replied in a strangled voice.

Barely slept, huffed his wolf.

"Can I sleep over with you both tonight?" asked the innocent little princess. "We can make a bed fort."

Ares wanted to laugh at Charly's expression. Time to save his lover. "You don't want to sleep in my room. I snore like a bear, remember? And so does your mom.

We're just sharing a bed so you could get a good night's sleep for the big day we've got planned."

"Oh." But Greta, being a kid with no filter, added, "Where did your pajamas go?"

"It was too hot," Charly squeaked.

"Tell you what, princess. Why don't you get your coat on and I'll be down in a second so we can go fetch some fresh eggs for breakfast?"

"Chickens. Yay!" She scampered off, and Charly pulled the covers over her head, muttering, "That was awkward."

"And we handled it. Although we might want to think about putting a bell on her to give us warning."

Charly peeked at him and scowled. "Not funny."

"It worked with the cat we used to have. Saved many birds that way."

"I didn't mean to fall asleep with you," she grumbled.

"But it happened, and I, for one, enjoyed it."

A mate belongs with her male.

Ares totally agreed.

Charly paused in the process of finding her clothes to toss him a soft smile over her shoulder. "I enjoyed it too. Although, if we're going to be sharing a bed, we should probably start making sure we put on pajamas."

"Deal!" He'd have agreed to anything to have her by his side.

"Speaking of dressing, you'd better get moving, or she will be back."

"On it." He hopped out of bed and threw on some clothes. He found Greta by the front door, pulling on her boots. Together, they entered the heated coop with the clucking hens, who cooperated with the raiding of the nests.

"Ares, look at this big one!" Greta held up a super-sized egg.

"Nice! I'll bet it makes good eggnog."

"Make?" Greta squished her nose. "You buy eggnog in the store."

"I like mine fresh. Later we'll make some with the eggs we gathered, and we'll milk Lottie the goat."

"Ooh, can I try that?"

"Of course, princess."

Hand in hand, they entered the kitchen, only to find Charly on her phone, looking pale.

"Look, Mama, so many eggs."

Charly smiled weakly. "That's awesome, munchkin."

"Why don't you put the eggs in the container." He pointed to the tray his mom kept on the counter. As Greta went off with the basket, he sidled close to Charly. "What is it?"

Charly gave a panicked look in Greta's direction. He caught the hint. "Hey, Greta, I'm in the mood for strawberry jam. I'm gonna see if the pantry has any."

"Mmm. I love jam," Greta exclaimed, clapping her hands.

"Charly, can you help me find it?" he asked, even as

he tugged her into the room and let the door swing close. Only then did he whisper, "What's wrong?"

She held out her phone. "I just got a call from my landlord. Apparently, my house was broken into last night."

"Fuck." The expletive slipped out. "Did they take anything?"

"He couldn't tell but said they trashed the place." Her lips trembled. "Who would do such a thing?"

"Assholes who probably heard about the evacuation because of the fire," his easy reply. "I'll check out the damage after breakfast."

"No, I'll go. I'm going to call in sick to work. Can you hang with Greta? I don't want her seeing the destruction." She clutched the phone so tight her knuckles turned white.

Good point, only he didn't want Charly dealing with this alone. With Selene and Mom gone, that left him with one option. "Let me call my sister Athena."

"We can't impose—"

He cut her off. "This isn't imposing. This is a family emergency, and before you say you're not family, I will disagree."

"Just because we had sex—"

"Made love," he corrected, to which his wolf added, *Mated*. "And it's more than that. Even if we weren't lovers, I'd still consider us friends. And friends help each other."

"She won't mind?" asked in a little voice.

"Let's find out." Before he could call, Greta poked her head into the pantry. "What's taking so long?"

He grabbed a jar of jam and held it up. "Found it! I have to phone my sister, but would you mind toasting me two pieces of bread?"

"With jam?" Greta asked.

"Heck yeah. Butter first, then lots of jam," he said with a wink.

"On it," Greta chirped.

"I'll help." Charly followed her to the counter with the toaster while Ares stepped into the living room and called his sister.

Athena answered after the second ring. "Good morning. Kind of early to be calling, though."

"I need a favor."

Without hesitation, she replied, "Sure."

"A strange one."

"Okay."

Had to love his sister. No questions asked, just ready to help. "I need you to watch Greta—she's my friend's kid—while her mom and I check out some damage caused by some overnight vandals at her place. They're staying at the farm right now because a neighbor's place caught on fire and they need to inspect the townhouse unit for damage."

"I know," she stated.

"How?"

"Mom, duh. Because it's not like my only brother ever calls."

He cleared his throat. "I was busy."

"I'll bet you were. Anyhow, as to the kid, I can watch her but, rather than bring her to my place, meet me at the Arnprior fire station."

"Why?" he asked.

"Because they're having a Christmas celebration thing for all the firefighters' kids. Derek volunteered to help. Grams baked a whack of stuff for it. Rumor has it Santa is supposed to show."

"Shit, that sounds awesome. Let me run it by Charly."

"Run what by me?" she queried, having entered the living room.

"Athena wants to know if Greta can go to the Christmas party at the firehall. Her boyfriend, Derek, is helping out with it, and it's gonna have activities and stuff."

"She'll keep a close eye on her?" Charly chewed her lower lip.

Athena heard. "Tell her I will bite anyone that lays a hand on her kid."

He changed it to, "Says she'll guard Greta with her life."

Charly nodded. "Okay. What time does it start?"

"Ten," Athena replied. "But we'll be there before nine setting up."

"Okay, we'll do breakfast and get dressed then head over."

Greta was quite excited not only to attend a party,

but also to meet Ares' other sister. On the ride over, Charly handed her phone over to her daughter with instructions to call Ares if she got scared or uncomfortable.

Greta, in true kid fashion, which foreshadowed her teen years, rolled her eyes. "Yes, Mama. I'll be fine." Greta might be, but Charly was a wreck.

Her expression remained wan when she met Athena. Her smile forced when she said goodbye to Greta and told her to have fun.

As they drove over to the townhouse, he held Charly's hand tight.

"It will be okay."

"Not really. We already had so little."

"You're not alone," he promised as he squeezed her fingers.

"Thank you for coming with me. I feel so discombobulated right now."

"Holy big word. And let me say, you're doing better than me. I would have probably gotten drunk."

She snorted. "Such a guy solution."

"Don't knock it 'til you've tried it."

The moment they pulled into her place the damage was visible. The front window smashed—from the inside, according to the shards on the front lawn. Rudolph had been utterly destroyed, its head torn from the body and then stomped.

The interior looked as if someone had taken a bat to everything. Not a single piece of furniture remained intact. Ceramic and glass shards littered the kitchen. The fridge had been left open, and the little food inside tossed to the floor. Cupboard doors ripped off. The Christmas tree had been knocked over and...

Someone marked the tree.

No way. He took a second sniff. His wolf was right. Some fucker had pissed on it.

It wasn't the only thing soaked in urine. Charly stood staring at her bed, which had a pile of shit in the middle, along with soaked sheets. She turned deathly pale when she entered the bathroom and saw on the mirror, written in lipstick, *Whore.*

Charly uttered a whimper.

Protect! Wolf insisted.

"We've seen enough," he stated, tugging her by the hand.

"I can't go. I have to clean up and—"

"Everything is trash," he said, more harshly than necessary. Blame his impotent rage at the vandals who'd hurt his Charly.

Her eyes brimmed with tears.

"Don't cry," he said, softening his tone. "I didn't mean to sound like an asshole. I'm pissed at whoever did this. Who the fuck destroys someone's home?"

"I can think of someone," her soft murmur.

He stared at her. "Wait, you think this is your ex?"

She shrugged. "It's possible. I mean, why would a random stranger be so mad?"

This went beyond mad into vindictive and cruel.

Before he could reply, they heard a man holler from downstairs, "Ms. Dawson, are you here?"

"Yes, Mr. Rodriguez. Coming down."

Ares followed Charly to the main floor to find her landlord standing with his arms crossed. "This place is uninhabitable."

"I'm sorry. I obviously had no idea this would happen when the fire marshal told me to leave until they checked the structure."

"Not your fault, but this..." Mr. Rodriguez waved. "This is too much damage. You can't live here anymore."

Her mouth rounded. "But my rent is paid."

"I will reimburse this month and return your last month's rent," her landlord insisted. "This will take weeks, maybe months, to fix."

"He's right," Ares murmured softly. "The whole place needs to be gutted."

"It's only days before Christmas. Where am I supposed to go?" Charly's voice broke.

"Do you really have to ask?" he replied.

Her eyes shone with tears, and her lips wobbled. "It's too much."

"No, it's not. I've got you, Charly."

Indeed, he held her up, as her whole body appeared on the verge of collapse. It didn't help that the intruder left nothing intact. The meager clothing she'd not taken with her, ruined. Not just torn, but also pissed on, and by more than one person. Three by his count. The presents she'd tucked in her closet? Trampled and destroyed, which left her shaking. He didn't need to ask to know what she thought.

What will I have for Greta on Christmas?

What would she tell Greta?

Not the truth. A child that young would be traumatized by something this violent.

They exited the townhouse, his arm holding her upright, her head ducked, but his remained high and alert, which was how he spotted the rental car a few doors up. Someone slouched in the front seat.

Could be a coincidence, but the raised hairs on his nape—and his wolf's growled *Enemy*—said otherwise.

While he couldn't confront them, not in front of witnesses and most especially Charly, he could take precautions, such as making sure they couldn't follow. Luckily, Charly was too overwrought to notice the circuitous route he took to lose their tail. It helped he drove them out of Arnprior into Kanata.

When he pulled into the Toys R Us parking lot, she finally lifted her head and muttered, "Why are you parking here? We need to go get Greta."

"We will, right after we make sure she has presents under the tree."

"What tree?" her bitter reply.

"The one we're going to cut down this afternoon and decorate."

She blinked at him.

"It won't be Chevy Chase-sized, but I have a nice

one that will look great in the living room. I know where the ornaments and lights are. Although I'm thinking we should get Greta a new decoration, something special she can hang. Oh, and we'll need to get her a holiday hat. We've got a couple at the house, but I'd like to get her a pink princess one."

She kept staring.

"What? You don't like the idea of a pink one? I guess we could do traditional red or green elf."

She flung herself at him and mashed her mouth to his, whispering, "What did I do to deserve you?"

"Ever think it's the other way around?"

"I'll repay you," she promised.

"Oh shut it. This isn't about money. I have plenty in the bank. This is about making sure that little girl has an epic Christmas. You in?"

Finally, a real smile curved her lips. "Yes."

They did some serious damage in Toys R Us. When Charly would have gotten the cheap generic fashion doll, he insisted on the fancy name brand Barbie Special Holiday Edition. When she would have stopped at three gifts, he laughed. "My princess is getting spoiled." And so was her mother; she just didn't know it yet. Although he didn't have much time. He kind of regretted now telling Selene to go on that cruise. He could have used her as his Secret Santa shopper. At least he had Athena, who would probably roundly curse him if he sent her out last-minute gift scrounging, but she'd forgive him when she heard why.

With what happened at the townhouse, he couldn't leave the girls alone. He'd already sent Athena a text with instructions to not let Greta out of her sight with a quick explanation. Essentially, *Someone is after Charly and princess. Trust no one but family.*

Her reply, a wolf's head.

Whoever messed with Charly had fucked up bad, because if there was one thing you didn't do? Touch a wolf's mate and his pup.

Yes, his.

Because one thing had become crystal clear in the last few days.

Charly was the one.

CHAPTER 10

Charlotte didn't have the strength to fight Ares and his extravagance. How could she when he wanted to spoil Greta? Pride was one thing, but getting in the way of her kid having nice things? Her ego took a back seat. Greta deserved this. Heck, so did she.

Seeing the destruction at her place had broken something inside her. She'd thought herself safe. Wrong. Thought she could start over. Wrong. Thought she could do it alone. She could, but it would be easier if she had a partner. She tired of struggling. Wanted someone she could lean on during tough times. Deserved security and love.

Yes, love. She couldn't deny what burgeoned between her and Ares. It was more than attraction. More intense by a zillion than what she'd felt for Barry.

The quickness of how she fell for him frightened.

Opening her heart, letting him in, was one thing. She could—eventually—handle the heartbreak, but what about Greta? She'd formed such a strong bond with him already. What if Charlotte trusted wrong and her precious munchkin got hurt?

Hard to even imagine Ares would do such a thing, judging by his giddy excitement as he chose pink wrapping paper with unicorns being ridden by Santa, or when he held up an ornament in the shape of a crown with the name Greta etched on it.

"You're insane," she said, shaking her head as they checked out.

"Yup. And I'm okay with it." He reached out to grab her hand. "We are going to make sure princess has the best Christmas ever."

With shopping done, they drove back to Arnprior. She noticed him staring at every car they passed and how he kept checking his rearview mirror.

"What's wrong?" she asked because this wasn't the laidback Ares she'd come to know.

"Nothing."

"Ares..." She used her mom tone.

He broke immediately. "There was a rental parked in front of your place, and it followed us a few blocks before I lost it."

"What?" The blood in her veins froze.

"It might have just been a coincidence. Arnprior isn't a big place, so we might have been going in the same direction."

Her fingers clenched into fists. "What if it was…" She couldn't say her ex's name because, like a horror movie, it might just conjure him.

"Even if it was, you don't have to worry. You're safe with me. I won't let anyone hurt you or Greta."

She wanted to believe him, but Ares didn't know what Barry was capable of. She herself hadn't realized the dark side to him until he'd come around demanding she and Greta move in with him. The fact he'd suddenly decided to acknowledge her as his daughter had not been the joyful moment she'd hoped for; more like a nightmare.

Her silence led to him adding, "Seriously, Charly, I don't want you stressing about it."

"You're telling a mom whose kid might be in danger to not stress?" she exclaimed.

"Okay, you stress. I'll keep us safe." He pulled into the fire station and glanced at her. "I know this sounds dickish, but you might want to try and smile if you don't want Greta to sense you're worried."

She gave him a feral grin. "How's this?"

"Terrifying." He laughed.

She sighed. "Thanks for being honest."

"I debated not saying anything, but you need to know so you can be cautious. Not that we'll be leaving the farm for a few days. Weather forecast shows a big storm rolling in tonight, and it's supposed to linger until Boxing Day. Everything's gonna be closed since the roads will be a mess and no one will be able to get anywhere."

"Will we be okay? Do we need to stock up on anything?"

"We'll be fine. If the power goes out, then we've got the fireplace to keep us warm and plenty of candles. I'm a master at roasting wieners on an open flame."

"I know a better place to roast it." The words slipped out, and he laughed.

"My naughty Charly."

My? She liked the way he spoke possessively. "And you really don't mind us staying with you?"

"Nope. Guess you're stuck with me."

"Such a chore..." She uttered a dramatic sigh.

"Ouch."

Her turn to laugh. "Okay, so maybe it won't be complete torture."

"Killing me here."

She put her hand on his thigh for a squeeze. "I appreciate everything you're doing for me and Greta."

"And I appreciate the fact you've allowed me into your life. I'm really glad we met, Charly."

"So am I." She truly was.

"Shall we go fetch the princess and take her home?"

Home. It had a nice ring to it.

They entered the firehall to blasting Christmas music and found Greta getting ready to descend the pole. Despite the tumbling mats all around, Athena stood positioned at the bottom, ready to catch Greta if she slipped.

Charlotte did her best to not gasp and freak. The last thing she wanted was to curb her daughter's fearless spirit, but her stomach did tighten when Greta slid down squealing.

Greta landed on her feet and immediately spotted her. "Mama!" she cried, racing for her.

"Hey, munchkin. Are you having fun?"

A rapid head bob and a toothy grin followed by a gush of words. "So much fun! We had pizza and purple juice and chips. Santa came, too!"

Charlotte approached Athena with Ares by her side. "Hi, thanks again for giving us a hand with Greta."

"My pleasure. She's an absolute treasure." Athena then murmured, "And don't you worry about a thing. Ares is good at keeping those he cares about safe."

Charlotte's eyes widened.

Ares cleared his throat. "I told Athena about our possible situation."

"Just so you know, we didn't have any strangers pop by during the party. We kept an eye open."

"Thanks."

"You heading back to the farm?" Athena asked.

"Yeah, going to hunker down before the storm hits."

"You know, if you need a more secure place to stay, there's tons of room at the Kennedys'. Grams and Gramps have got cameras all over, and if the power goes out, they've got a generator to keep things running."

"Which is a hint we should get one at the house. I know." Ares grimaced. "Damned things are pricey." He glanced at Charlotte. "We have two small ones, but they're hooked to the barn and chicken coop to make sure the animals don't freeze during a power failure."

"Does it happen often?"

"We're in the country, so more often than we'd like, but we usually manage just fine. But given all that's going on, it might not be a bad idea to head to Grams and Gramps'."

"I couldn't impose," Charlotte murmured.

Athena snorted. "Oh, don't worry. If you're not welcome, they'll come right out and say it. But I guarantee they won't kick you out. For one, they like Ares, for two, despite their ornery act, they're actually very giving and caring people."

"They are," Ares stated. "I'll never forget how they helped my family out when we had our own situation."

"What happened?" Charlotte asked.

"Some unsavory folks had their sights on my sisters. Grams, Gramps, and their grandson, Derek, helped us to convince them to bother someone else."

Charlotte got the impression he glossed over the details. She doubted, though, that people harassing his sisters compared to a violent ex who'd kill her if she didn't give him what he wanted. "I wouldn't want to bring trouble to their doorstep."

For some reason, Athena laughed. "That would actually be the best present you could give them. Grams and Gramps thrive on drama and are the kind of folks ready for the apocalypse. They have a bomb shelter stocked to the rafters just in case."

"Their place really is more secure than the farm," Ares added.

"You think we should go?"

"I want you to be able to relax, and honestly, with Athena, Derek, Grams, and Gramps all keeping an eye out, ain't no one getting close to you or Greta."

Her kid's safety was more important than anything. Charlotte nodded. "Okay then, but only if they agree."

"They will. I'll let Grams know you'll be coming to stay until the storm passes and we know the house has power."

Ares glanced at Athena. "Sounds good. Can you take Greta with you? Charly and I will go home to pack some bags and make sure the house is ready for the storm then head over."

Only Greta didn't like that plan. Not the part about sleeping at a different house, though she was excited to see a new place. Greta eyed Ares, and her lower lip jutted as she said, "You said we'd cut down a special tree."

Ares glanced at Charlotte. "It won't take long to saw it down and load it onto the truck."

"What about the rest of the stuff that needs to get done?" she countered.

"The animals just need their automatic feeders topped up, a bit of antifreeze in the drains, water shut off and drained. If you can pack us some clothes while I'm doing that, then we'll be done within the hour."

"Okay," Charlotte agreed.

"Yay!" Greta clapped.

Before they loaded Greta into the car, Ares and Derek transferred the gifts they'd bought to Athena's car. Charlotte emerged with Greta to see Ares whispering with his sister and wondered why Athena's brows rose. Was he hiding something from her?

Athena hugged him and then waved at Charlotte. "See you in a few hours."

Greta thankfully chattered nonstop all the way to the farm and didn't notice how Ares kept watching his rearview mirror and took a more circuitous route back, even as the clouds darkened overhead.

No snow yet, but the heaviness of them indicated it would start falling soon.

Once they arrived at the house, Ares clapped his hands. "We're going to take my truck to the Kennedys' farm. For one, it has four-wheel drive, and two, we need the bed in the back of it to bring the tree."

"Can I help saw it down?" Greta asked.

"Yup, but first, let's make sure our animal friends are ready for the storm."

Greta kept him company while Charlotte packed their bags. She also put together a bag for Ares that included a hideous Christmas sweater she located in his closet. The fridge got its perishables put into a Styrofoam cooler she found in the pantry. She stacked everything by the front door and waited.

Waited anxiously as the first flakes began to fall. She probably worried for nothing. Even if Barry had found her new address, he'd never find them here, and even if he did, he wouldn't know they went to Derek's grandparents' place.

But what about after the storm? Where would they go? She couldn't live on other people's generosity forever.

She heard Ares and Greta before she saw them, singing a very loud version of "Jingle Bells." Stepping onto the porch, hugging her upper body, she could see them through the drifting snow. Greta with her red mittens, holding a branch on one side, Ares gripping the sawn trunk, doing the heavy dragging.

A grinning child exclaimed, "We cut down the most beautiful tree, Mama."

"I see that. It's going to be perfect," Charlotte agreed.

"Go see if your mama needs help while I get this loaded." Ares sent Greta into the house.

"I've got our stuff ready," she told her daughter. "Why don't you grab a quick snack then have a pee before we go?"

"Okay, Mama."

Greta skipped off, and Charlotte put on her jacket and boots to help load their stuff on to the truck. The cooler went in the bed among the tree boughs. The bags in the backseat, leaving a spot for Greta's car seat. She'd just latched it in place when Ares growled, "Get in the house."

"What?" She glanced at him and noticed he stared up the driveway.

"Someone's coming. Get inside. Stay away from the windows."

Suddenly frightened, she hustled her butt, even as she tried to convince herself to stick around and show support. Ares sounded so serious though, and honestly, what use would she be?

It was probably nothing. Ares had made sure no one followed them. No one knew she was here, not even her work.

Despite his warning, she planned to watch from the window behind the curtain, only Greta called for her. "Mama, my hands are too sticky to turn on the water."

"Coming, munchkin."

She washed Greta from the honey she'd eaten with

her crackers. Then ensured she went potty. By the time she returned to the front of the house, the visitor had gone, but a grim Ares muttered, "Time to get going."

"Who was it?" she asked.

"Trouble."

CHAPTER 11

Ares remained on high alert the entire time he prepped the farm and fetched the tree with Greta. As he finished strapping the fir into the bed of his truck, he heard a car turning into the driveway. Not suspicious in and of itself. Sometimes people got lost or needed to turn around. Mom's honey shack, at the top of the driveway, also led to some seeking it after it closed for the season. Still, not wanting to take a chance, Ares sent Charly inside as a precaution.

Good thing

First off, the car that slowed to a stop a few meters from his truck had rental plates. It differed in style and color from the one he'd seen that morning outside Charly's place, though. The guy that emerged from the driver's seat had size to him, not the kind that came from muscle, but excess. While not fat, his body bore some extra padding. Dark hair with matching beard. A lumberjacket layered over a knitted sweater. Jeans and steel-toe boots.

His wolf growled, *Bad. Bad. Bad.*

He'd already figured that part out.

Ares strolled in the stranger's direction. "Can I help you?"

"Looking for Ares' Artisanal Cheese."

The mention of his company surprised. For one, while he advertised his business, he didn't offer an address. His cheese was sold mostly at farmers' markets and by special arrangement with small vendors in the area.

"Who's asking?"

"I'm looking for the owner. Ares McMurray."

"I'm Ares."

"You're the cheesemaker?" Buddy eyed him up and down with a smirk. "You don't look like a pansy."

That arched his brow. "Funny you should say that. I thought you looked like a dick, and here you are sounding like one."

The insult drew the stranger's brows together. "Do you try and piss off everyone who comes looking to buy your artsy-fartsy cheese?"

"Only those who shouldn't be here. I don't sell cheese from my house, so I'm kind of wondering how you got my address."

"Wasn't too hard to find, given you're a registered business." A claim that indicated this guy went through the trouble.

"What do you want?" Ares didn't even pretend to be polite. Something about the fellow had his wolf growling, *Enemy.*

"I'm looking for a woman and her daughter. My wife to be exact. We had a tiff, and she ran off."

Ares didn't let his expression change. "I'm sure it had nothing to do with your shining personality."

"Don't fuck with me. Have you seen them?"

"Why would I have seen them?" Ares lied. "I'm single and kind of happy to stay that way."

"Your business card was found where she's staying."

The admission almost sent him the few remaining feet separating them so he could pummel the man's smug face. This asshole had been the one to trash Charly's place.

He held himself in check. While hitting would offer some satisfaction, it wouldn't keep his girls safe.

Rather than give anything away, he scoffed at the guy's assumption. "Lots of people have my cards. I hand out hundreds every summer at the farmers' markets."

"Says the guy whose truck was spotted on her street." The guy glanced at Ares' vehicle.

"Where abouts does your wife live?"

"Arnprior."

Ares shook his head. "Haven't been to Arnprior in about a month. And hate to break it to you, but my truck's hardly unique."

"You don't want to be keeping my wife and kid from me," warned the fellow.

"Wouldn't dream of it, only I don't have them, and if you can't find them, maybe there's a reason."

The guy took an aggressive step in his direction. "You need to watch what you say."

"Or what?" Ares broadened his shoulders and let a mean glint enter his eyes. "Gonna hit me? Go ahead. But be warned, I will hit back harder."

Much harder.

The man's lips pursed. "If I find out you're hiding them…"

"Oh fuck off already. Your wife and kid ain't here, and I got better shit to deal with than an asshole."

"Going somewhere?"

"None of your fucking business. Now git."

The belligerent man got into his car, a surprise, as Ares really thought he'd fight. The asshole reversed and turned around before speeding off, kicking up gravel and snow.

Ares kept watching, and listening, even after his wolf said, *He's gone.*

Gone, but he shouldn't have come here in the first place. He'd completely forgotten he'd given Charly his business card. Good thing they weren't planning to stay. Although they would have to eventually come back. Even with the feeders and the heaters, he'd have to return to check the animals within a day or so. He'd have to do something about the asshole before then.

When the girls did emerge, he couldn't help glancing up the driveway. Had the jerk parked out of sight? Would they be ambushed?

Ares hated saying anything, but Charly had a right to know. When he told her they had trouble, her expression became that scared, panicked look he hated so much.

Protect, whined his wolf.

I'm trying.

"What kind of trouble?" she murmured.

"Hold on a second while I get Greta buckled." He put the kid in her booster and handed her a book he'd bought earlier that day, a find-the-object picture book that had her "Ooohing."

"You stay in here where it's nice and toasty, while your mom and me finish locking up."

Greta was already engrossed as he closed the truck door.

"Who was in the car?" Charly hissed.

"Your ex I assume, since he called you his wife."

She snorted. "We were never married. We lived together for just over a year. We weren't even engaged." As her ire faded, she whispered, "He found us."

"He doesn't know that. He came here because he found my business card at your place, so I told him to fuck off, that I didn't know you."

"He won't give up." She paced in a tight circle and wrung her hands.

"Don't you worry about that prick. I'll handle him."

"You can't. You don't understand what he's capable of." She paused before blurting out, "He's killed people."

Not surprising given his brutish thug vibe. "And?"

"And I don't want you to be hurt."

"Aw, Charly." He grabbed her hands and forced her to meet his gaze. "You don't have to worry about me. I guarantee you I'm tougher than that fucker."

Way tougher. And meaner. Full moon is soon. We should eat his face.

He just might, if only to get that petrified look off her face.

"Are you not listening? I just said he's killed people."

He dropped a kiss on the tip of her nose. "Still not worried and neither should you be. Have I mentioned Grams and Gramps are marksmen? Oh, and they have their property booby-trapped, which is in addition to all the cameras."

"I don't want them shooting Barry and going to jail."

"As if the cops would ever find a body," he scoffed, only belatedly realizing how it sounded.

She blinked at him.

He smiled. "Just kidding. If your ex comes intending violence, then we have a right to defend ourselves."

"Maybe in the USA, but this is Canada. You're more likely to be arrested than him," she grumbled.

She had a point. Their justice system could be skewed in favor of criminals. "Maybe he'll try to come through the woods, and something even meaner will eat him."

A ghost of a smile curved her lips. "We should be so lucky."

Little did she know he could make it a reality. Animal attacks, while rare this close to the city, did happen, and if a stranger dumbly met a wolf and succumbed to his injuries, well, that was nature.

Hunting time?

Soon. Very soon. The full moon would be coming, and while he could shift without it, he'd be at his strongest during its glow. If he could sneak away. It might actually be easier in a house full of people. He could always use the excuse he had to check on the farm.

"Come on. Let's get out of here before the storm worsens." The falling snow had thickened while they talked, covering the ground in a layer of white.

"Is it safe to drive?" she asked.

"We'll be fine. It's not too far from here." The truth, in good weather.

What should have taken under forty minutes took over an hour. While his truck in four-by-four could handle the slick conditions, other people couldn't. They saw three cars in the ditch before they left the highway. Two more with their hazards flashing as they hit the country road to Grams and Gramps' place. However, this wasn't his first snowy rodeo. They made it there safely.

Ares hopped out of the truck, but before he could give Charly a hand, she was standing in the creeping snow, looking around. "Big farm."

"Yeah. They've got a few more acres than us." A hundred more, to be exact.

He reached up for Charly, who slid into his arms with a giggle. "Is this Athena's house?" Greta pointed to the structure with the wrap-around porch.

"Kind of. Remember Derek? He grew up with his grandparents here."

"I don't have a grandma," Greta informed him.

"Well, I think the Grams Kennedy will be happy to let you think of her as one while you're here." He winked as he put her on the ground. "Head up to the house while I grab our bags."

Greta happily skipped through the snow, but Charly gave him a hand. "You're sure we're not imposing?"

"Athena texted they were expecting us. But be warned, the Kennedys are kind of nutty."

"Nutty how?"

"Well, they cuss a lot."

Charly grimaced. "Not ideal, but I can handle it."

"And they love to talk about the coming apocalypse."

"You mentioned the bomb shelter. Guess that makes them preppers."

"Of the highest order. Also, they grow cannabis."

Her eyes widened. "As in weed?"

"Yes."

Her lips pursed in disapproval, and he hastened to add, "It is completely legal. Grams and my mom actually have a collaboration. THC-infused honey. They're thinking of branching out into edibles since they both love to cook."

"I don't do drugs."

"This isn't a drug den, I promise. While Gramps does edibles for his arthritis, Grams doesn't touch the stuff."

"Guess it's too late to go home now," she muttered.

"It will be fine. You'll see. They're actually quite sweet once you get past the fact Grams calls Derek the little bastard."

"Isn't he her grandson?"

"Yeah. But I promise it's a term of endearment."

Charly sighed. "Anything else?"

"Expect to see guns. For protection, you know, from like bears and stuff."

"Guns." A flat repeat of the word.

"Don't worry. They won't have them where Greta can play with them, and the safeties will be on."

"Greta knows better than to touch them. We had a big talk about guns after a classmate in BC accidentally shot themselves with their dad's service weapon."

"Yikes."

"Indeed." She squared her shoulders. "Okay, let's do this."

They marched to the house. Athena had already ushered Greta inside and, as they entered, was showing the princess where to hang her coat and put her boots. He didn't remember seeing the kid-height hook last time he was there.

"Storm's getting bad," Athena observed, glancing outside before shutting the door behind them.

"Roads are already showing accumulation and idiots," he advised. "Where's Derek?"

"Out in the barn with the horses. He wanted to give them some extra oats, and then he's going to run a guideline from the barn to the house in case visibility is poor in the morning."

"Horses?" Greta picked up on the word, and Athena grinned as she crouched.

"Yup. We also have a cow for milk, pigs, and chickens."

"Ares has goats."

"I know. Who do you think buys the pajamas for them?" Athena winked.

"What happened to Rosy?" Ares had gotten used to the old hound greeting him with a woof.

"Rainbow bridge," Athena murmured.

"Damn, she was a good dog." Ares didn't have one

growing up because his mom said she already had enough canines in the house.

"Shall we go meet Grams and Gramps?" Athena asked.

Greta nodded, but she snagged her mother's hand as they entered the living room.

"About time you got here. Gramps was about to fire up the snowmobile and go hunting for you," declared Grams from her throne, a plaid-covered recliner. The footrest had been elevated to accommodate one of her knees bound in bandages.

"Hey, Grams, what happened to the leg?" Ares asked upon seeing her.

"Twisted it when I slipped on some ice," her scowled reply.

"And she won't take anything for the pain," Gramps added from a matching chair. The pair might be in their seventies but appeared and acted younger. They had the grayish-white hair of age and a face full of wrinkles, but both remained very active.

"Grams, I'd like you to meet my friend, Charlotte, and her highness, princess Greta."

"Hello and thank you for inviting us into your home," a polite Charly stated.

"Bah, it's no problem. Plenty of room, although we do expect everyone to pull their weight," Grams stated.

"Yes, ma'am."

"Don't call me ma'am," Grams squeaked. "I'm Grams, this is Gramps."

Gramps grunted.

Charly leaned down to whisper to Greta, "Say hello."

"Hi." A shy Greta tucked behind her mom.

"I once knew a Greta," Grams stated. "Loved chocolate chip cookies."

Greta peeked out from behind a leg. "So do I."

"It just so happens I've got all the ingredients to make a fresh batch in the kitchen. With this bum knee, I could use a helper. I don't suppose you like to cook?"

"I love to cook." Greta emerged with a smile.

As Grams went to heave herself from the chair, Ares dove to give her a hand and got a glare for daring to offer.

"I'm not an invalid yet," Grams grumbled. Her expression brightened as she tottered around Ares. "Come with me, sweetling. Let's go make those cookies, and we'd better hide some for Santa, else Gramps will gobble them all up."

Derek walked in just as Grams left the room with Greta. Ares stared in shock, and Derek's jaw dropped, but Athena snickered.

Charlotte eyed them with confusion. "Is something wrong?"

"Grams never talks that nice," Derek stated.

"Or without swearing," Ares added.

Athena smirked. "Guess someone's got a soft spot for kids."

"A good thing, since you're expecting," Ares stated.

Athena pursed her lips. "Says who?"

"As if I wouldn't notice the changes in you," he scoffed.

Gramps chuckled. "We all knew. Grams is already ordering stuff for the nursery."

Athena shook her head but smiled as she patted her belly. "You are going to be so spoiled."

"Heck yes, she is!" Ares rubbed his hands. "Uncle Ares is going to be her favorite."

"How do you figure?"

"I have goats."

"Selene has bunnies," Athena pointed out.

"I make cheese."

"Fancy cheese. Kids like the orange stuff in plastic or a jar," Athena riposted.

"She's right," Charly added. "Greta loves that processed stuff."

"I will be the favorite," Ares insisted.

"Nah, that will be me," Derek argued. "She's gonna be daddy's girl."

"You're all idiots," Gramps blustered. "She's gonna be grandpa's angel, you'll see."

Charlotte leaned close as they continued to argue. "This isn't what I expected."

"Better or worse?"

"Kind of awesome. It's obvious everyone's real close to each other."

"Family isn't always about blood. It's who you can tolerate," he sagely stated.

"Should I give Grams a hand?" she asked, looking at the kitchen.

Athena heard and shook her head. "You'll get in Grams' bad books for sure if you do. Helping is by invitation only. Why don't we get your stuff up to your rooms? Grams gave you the corner bedroom with the queen bed, and Greta's right across the hall in the hobby room with the futon."

"There must be something I can do to help, though," Charly insisted once they returned downstairs from dropping their bags in the room.

Gramps cleared his throat. "I hear someone brought a tree. You could get started on that."

The tree went up in the front window—after they smacked most of the snow from its branches—and a dusty box of ornaments emerged from a storage closet under the basement stairs.

A beaming Greta emerged right after they wrapped the tree in lights, carefully balancing a tray of hot cookies. Grams, wearing the softest smile Ares had ever seen, hobbled after her.

"The girl is a natural chef," Grams declared, sitting in her chair once more. Everyone took a cookie or two —or three, in Ares' case—and agreed.

To everyone's surprise, Greta ended up in Grams'

lap, where the two of them put their heads together and discussed what they'd bake Christmas Eve.

Charly leaned against Ares and whispered, "I'm so glad you convinced me to come."

So was he, especially once the storm took out the power for a good chunk of Ottawa and surrounding areas.

Once Greta went to bed—after hugging Grams, Gramps, Athena, and Derek—things got serious as Grams stared at Charly and point-blank asked, "Who's the asshole terrorizing you and that sweet child?"

CHAPTER 12

At Charlotte's shocked look, Grams added, "Yes, I know you're being threatened."

"I'm sorry. I shouldn't have come," Charlotte whispered. These nice people didn't deserve to get dragged into her mess.

"Oh, stop it with that bullshit. Of course, you should be here. This is the safest place you could be. So can the bullshit and spill. Ares didn't tell us much, and I'd rather hear the details from you."

Charlotte wrung her hands. "It's my ex. He followed me from British Columbia."

"I'm going to assume he's a shitty father since you're trying to keep him away from the kid?" Grams didn't pull punches.

"He abandoned her at three months old. Tried claiming she wasn't his, and when a paternity test showed she was, he called her defective." Charlotte clenched her fists as the familiar hot anger filled her. "There is nothing wrong with Greta."

"I take it he changed his mind?" Athena's soft addition.

"About eight months ago, he showed up unexpectedly. Barged his way into our apartment, demanded to see Greta. She'd already gone to bed, and I refused to wake her up. When I asked what he wanted, he told me to hand her over."

"That's insane," Athena huffed. "He can't have seriously expected you to comply."

"I told him he was nuts and to get out, that he'd relinquished his parental rights. I reminded him that he called her defective, and he smirked. Told me he'd changed his mind and either we moved in with him or he'd take Greta."

"No court would have agreed," Derek stated.

"He wasn't planning to do it legally." Her hand went to her cheek. "And he gave me a taste of what to expect if I didn't give in." Charlotte saw how Ares' jaw clenched as he simmered with anger on her behalf. Honestly, the slap, while it stung, hadn't hurt as much as the thought of losing Greta.

"After the assault, you left BC and came here," Derek stated.

"Not right away. I hoped I could reason with Barry. Offered him supervised visits on the weekend so as to ease him into her life."

"Wait, you actually were going to let him see her?" Ares couldn't help his shock.

Charlotte shrugged. "He's her father. I owed it to Greta to give him a chance."

"He wasn't content with the offer," Grams surmised.

"Not one bit. He wanted us under his control. And he got it. For two weeks."

Ares stiffened. "You agreed to live with him?"

"Not exactly. He kidnapped us, took us to a remote house in the woods, and made it so we couldn't escape." That had been the toughest moment of her life. Kept locked in a room, allowed out only under supervision. She'd done her best to keep Greta from realizing the severity of their situation, but she knew. She'd smiled very little. Spent a lot of time huddled on Charlotte's lap.

"You obviously got away," Athena pointed out.

"By fluke. When he and his gang went out one night, I smashed the handle off the door of the room he kept us in." Her lips twisted as she offered a wry, "I couldn't figure out how to pick the lock. Luckily, he hates banks. I took a few thousand in cash and stole his car. Drove to the bus depot and ditched it. Then took a taxi to the train station and booked us some seats."

"You made him think you took a bus," Ares murmured. "Smart."

"We travelled by train and bus." Charlotte stood

and paced. "I'd planned to go farther east, but my emergency stash got too low, so we ended up here."

"When you say this asshole is violent, what are we talking about?" Grams questioned. "We know he's a piece of shit who likes to smack women, what else?"

Charlotte hesitated. "He's the leader of a gang or a cult depending on how you view it. Around a dozen or so men and women who live in some cabins on his property. They intimidate local businesses for money."

"Protection scam," Derek murmured.

"It's blackmail, all right, as the money is to protect those folks from him and his gang." Charlotte paused and ducked her head before admitting, "He is a killer. On the day I escaped the cabin, he showed me his depraved side thinking it would make me fall in line. The victims hadn't done anything wrong, simply got lost, but rather than let them leave, they..." She swallowed hard. "He and his gang murdered them." The memory of the pleading, the blood, the screams still haunted her.

"I met Charly's ex," Ares announced. "He came by the farm before we left. Doesn't seem like he followed us here, but he's as you'd expect. A big, brutish bully."

"Did he bring his gang?" asked Derek.

Charlotte shrugged. "I don't know. He might have."

"He was driving a rental, which implies he flew in," Ares added to the information pot.

"I can't imagine it was cheap flying last minute this

close to Christmas, so unless he's willing to waste a ton of dough, I imagine he only brought a few of his posse. While he couldn't bring weapons through security, it wouldn't be that hard for him to pick something up from the black market," Athena's contribution.

Charlotte eyed them all. "You're taking this all very calmly." Sane people would have been on her to call the cops or leave so as to not bring her troubles to their doorstep.

A hard-eyed Grams spat, "I ain't calm. The thought of some asshole trying to hurt that sweet baby has me ready to hunt down that fucker and put a bullet between his eyes."

Charlotte's eyes widened, and Ares grabbed her hand. "I know that sounds harsh, but the reality is, guys like your ex can't be scared off with words."

Agreed, but still, murder? "You ran him off earlier today," she reminded.

"Because he wasn't sure you were with me, and I imagine because I was tougher than he expected. More than likely, he'll return with some of his bully boys to see if I was lying."

"Pity the roads are so shit. We could have lain in wait," Derek lamented.

"Maybe if he can't find me, he'll go away." Charlotte still hoped for a miracle.

"Don't you suddenly go dumb on me," Grams chided. "That man didn't follow you this far to give up. We'll have to be prepared. We'll get you set up with a gun."

"But I don't know how to shoot one," squeaked Charlotte.

"It's called aim and pull the trigger. Even if you miss, it will cause noise and bring others to help," Grams dry reply.

"And if I hit someone?" Charlotte asked faintly.

"I know how to clean blood so the cops can't find a trace." Grams wore a secretive smile.

"I don't want to kill anyone, and I don't want anyone to get arrested for murder," Charlotte exclaimed.

"Ain't murder," Grams stated. "It's what's needed to protect you and that sweet girl. And don't you worry about us getting caught. Can't charge us with murder if they don't have a body."

"Well, it's doubtful he'll find us here," Charlotte said, more to convince herself. "I should get to bed. Greta rises early."

"So do we." Grams pushed herself to her feet and hobbled to Charlotte. "You might not like our methods, but we will keep you safe."

With that, everyone went to their rooms, the one she and Ares shared not very large. Most of the space taken up by the queen-sized bed covered in a thick patchwork quilt. While fatigue did tug, Charlotte didn't lie down. She paced.

"I shouldn't have come. Oh god, what if Barry comes here and hurts them?" she lamented.

"Don't let Gram hear you. She's liable to give you a cuff." Ares tried to be light with his words, but she whirled with trembling lips.

"Barry will kill anyone who gets in his way."

"You're assuming we're easy to kill. I can tell you right now we're not." Ares wrapped his arms around her. "I wish you'd told me what he did to you. I mean I guessed it was bad, but Jeezus, Charly. You're lucky to be alive."

"I'm aware."

"You know he's not going to give up and go away. He's going to keep coming for you and Greta as long as he lives."

"I think about it every second of every day," she whispered against his chest.

"Then you know there's only one way to stop him."

What he implied... "Maybe he'll get arrested," her weak reply.

"These days he's more likely to get a slap on the wrist than go to prison."

How mad would Barry be if he went to jail because of her? "How can you speak about it so calmly? All of you acted as if killing people were an everyday thing."

"Not for me, but Grams and Gramps did fight in a war. I did warn you they weren't like other folk."

"Will they really kill Barry if he shows?"

"Most likely. They understand there's only one way to deal with that kind of man. The fact they are determined to act is a compliment. They don't like many people, and yet you've already won them over."

"You mean Greta did."

"Grams took a shine to you too. She's not usually that soft-spoken and polite."

Her eyes rounded. "That was polite?"

"You should hear her when she's herself. It's 'fuck this. Fuck that.' She was being so nice she didn't call Derek 'the little bastard' once."

"They're good people, but I meant what I said. I don't want them getting in trouble because of me."

"I'd say the chances of your ex showing are slim to none, so I wouldn't worry about it. But at least you know they're prepared, meaning you can sleep in peace. Ain't no one getting their hands on Greta."

That was probably the only thing that kept her from fleeing. These people genuinely cared and wanted to keep them safe. And truth be told, while the frank talk did discomfit, Ares and the others did have a point. Now that Barry had decided he wanted Greta, nothing would stop him but death. A terrible thing to think, this was her child's father. A scumbag who would traumatize a little girl who deserved better. A man who would most likely kill her if they ever met again.

"You're thinking too much," Ares murmured against the top of her head as he held her.

"Can you blame me?"

"Nah, stressing about the situation is understandable. Good thing I've got something that will fix that."

"Sleeping pills?"

"Nah, something better. You just need to get naked first."

Her mouth rounded. "You can't be serious."

"Very. Get your butt on the bed and get ready for the best massage of your life."

She wanted to argue. Wanted to keep tormenting herself. Instead, she stripped and lay face down on the bed.

Ares proceeded to knead her muscles. Working out the knots. Relaxing every inch of her until she felt something other than stress. When she flipped over and reached for him, he was ready.

To her surprise, making love eased even more of her tension. Afterward the intense orgasm, they snuggled, cozy under their pile of blankets, even too hot. The woodstoves in the house kept things toasty.

Ares spooned her from behind, their pajamas—which she'd insisted on them wearing—not really getting in the way of that snuggly intimacy. She fell asleep and woke to Greta beaming at them.

"Mama, wake up and come see all the snow."

So much snow. They'd gotten forty centimeters overnight, and it was still coming down.

It could have meant backbreaking shoveling, only

after the most ridiculous breakfast—fried potatoes, pancakes, bacon, sausage, toast, eggs, and even freshly squeezed orange juice—Derek got the tractor with its plow going, and the boys took turns chugging up and down the driveway. Greta whooped when they took her for a ride on it.

Greta played outside for hours, and so did Ares and Derek. They built her an epic snow fort and a maze in the snow to reach it.

Charlotte preferred the indoors and, after getting shooed from the kitchen, spent much time standing at the window watching.

Worrying.

And even praying.

Please, don't let anyone take my munchkin away.

CHAPTER 13

Ares could see Charlotte worried. Luckily, Greta didn't. Then again, they kept her busy. The dumping of snow, the sticky packing kind, made it perfect for building and—

"Snowball fight!" Athena's warning before she smacked him in the face with a nice toss.

"To the fort, princess," Ares shouted as he scooped Greta under one arm and ran for cover.

Greta giggled as they hunkered behind the wall of snow to avoid the next missile. "This is fun."

"This is war," he said with a waggle of his brows.

"I'll make snowballs for you to throw." She began scooping and patting the cold, wet stuff.

"Good thinking." As fast as Greta made them, Ares threw them at his sister, who stood in the open, laughing.

Derek, however, glowered.

"What's up, grumpy?" Athena asked.

"You're pregnant!"

"And? Doctors say exercise is good."

"Exercise, yes, not getting pummeled with snow," insisted her mate.

"Bah, Ares throws like a girl."

Ares stood. "He's got a point, sis. Preggos and kiddos should be off-limits."

"Okay." Athena got an impish smile. "But do you know who isn't?"

She whirled and hit Derek in the chest with a snowball.

He glanced at the white spot. "Seriously?"

"Better run for cover, sugar plum, because you are going down."

Rather than hide, Derek stalked for Athena, who kept grabbing snow and firing it. She managed three tosses before Derek got close enough to grab her and shove snow down the neck hole of her jacket.

"Eek!" Athena screamed. "That's cold." When he would have given her a snow job—which for the uninformed involved rubbing snow in someone's face—she cried, "Uncle! You win."

"As if there were any doubt." Derek smirked. "Once the baby is born, we can have the most epic snowball battle. But until then... get your sweet ass in the house and warm that fetus up. I'll wager Grams has some hot cocoa ready."

"Cocoa!" Ares lost his snowball-making partner as

Greta bolted to go find it, entering the house with Athena.

Derek lingered behind. "You think that fucker is going to show up?"

"I'd say there's a chance. He's wilier than I would have thought. He found my business card at Charly's and hunted down my home address."

"Sounds more like he got lucky. He won't know about Grams and Gramps' farm."

"Assuming he didn't follow me. Assuming he doesn't find out Athena is dating you. Assuming there's nothing at the farm that would give our location away." Ares had been racking his brain to think if they might have left a clue.

"You know, I really hate when the bad guys make the first move."

"What are you thinking?" Ares asked.

"Now that the storm's eased, what are the chances he goes back to your place, looking to cause trouble?"

"Depends on if he thinks I was lying before."

"We could head over to check on things," Derek suggested.

"The roads are shit and will be for hours." Which worked against and for them, as it meant Barry would have difficulty getting around.

"As if we'd drive anything with wheels," Derek scoffed.

"You mean take some snowmobiles?" Ares rubbed his chin. "Going cross country, we'd get there in decent time. The question is, should we both go? I hate leaving the girls unprotected."

Derek snorted. "You want to say that to Athena's face? With her hormones running wild, she's more dangerous than both of us put together. Not to mention, Grams might shoot you for even implying they can't handle a threat."

A rueful grin twisted Ares' lips. "Good point. Wanna head out after lunch? Gives us plenty of time to get there, see if anyone's been poking around, and be back in time for dinner."

"Sounds like a plan."

Hot chocolate awaited when they went inside, the homemade kind topped with marshmallows. The power failure hadn't impeded Grams' ability to cook with her gas stove. The toasty house didn't make the decision to go for a cold snowy ride easy, especially after he filled his belly with a savory soup and grilled cheese.

Nap time, his wolf suggested.

Not yet.

Ares wanted to see if Barry had returned to the farm and lay in wait. What if the fucker had and trashed his home? Hopefully, the asshole wouldn't go near the animals. That had been the one stumbling block with the plan to head to Grams and Gramps' to hunker down. Things could be replaced, but the animals they were responsible for had no defense.

He pulled Charly aside to let her know of his and

Derek's plan to visit the farm, but he framed it as them checking on the livestock and not seeing if Barry had returned.

Her lips pursed. "Is it safe? There's another storm system heading our way."

"It's not supposed to hit until after dinner. Plenty of time for us to get out there, check on things, and come back."

She brought up Barry. "What if *he's* there?"

"Doubtful. His rental didn't have all-wheel drive. If he even tried, he'd get stuck since our road is one the last plowed." Country living did have its drawbacks. "And before you wonder, he has no clue we're here. But even if by some weird chance he shows, just get into the bunker. Ain't no way he's getting to you in there. Leave him to stew and we'll handle him soon as we're back." The bomb shelter, once sealed, couldn't be opened from the outside without some serious metal-cutting tools.

Charly threw her arms around his neck. "Be careful."

"Don't you worry about me. I'll be fine. You go have some fun with the princess. I'll be back before you know it."

"Grams said I could be the co-assistant to the sous chef. I can't believe my kid ranks higher than me in the kitchen." Charly grimaced.

Ares grinned. "Count yourself lucky Grams even let you in her domain. I told you she likes you."

"If you say so." She kissed him, a soft lingering embrace where she murmured, "Come back to me."

"Always."

Just as they were suiting up to go, Ares' phone rang.

Selene called.

"Hey, little sis. How's the tropics treating you?"

"We never even made it off the ground," she announced.

"What?"

"The flight got delayed, and the storm hit before we could take off at our new time. They cancelled it and had us rebooked for this morning, but then that got pooched as well."

"Why didn't you call me?" he exclaimed.

"Because then you would have worried, duh."

"I am worried. The roads are shit. Stay in a hotel until they get them cleared."

"You're funny." She chuckled. "We're already home. Four-by-four all the way, baby. A little bit of snow wasn't going to stop me."

"You're at the house." Derek heard Ares and offered a sharp look.

"Yeah. Where else? Although I am wondering where you are."

"Grams and Gramps'. We got invited to spend Christmas since they have a generator."

"We really should get one of our own for the house. Can't believe your goats and the chickens get to keep warm while we make do with the woodstove in the living room."

Since he didn't know how to delicately broach it, he blurted out, "Did you see any signs of someone poking around?"

"No. Who would be crazy enough to be out in this weather?"

"Charly's ex. He popped by looking for her and Greta yesterday. I sent him off, but I'm not sure he believed me when I said I didn't know them. I was just going to head over because I was worried he might have returned and trashed our place like he did Charly's."

"Are Charly and Greta okay?"

"Yeah, they're fine. He didn't see them, but I don't think he'll give up that easily."

"I can see why you went to see Grams. She'll just shoot him if he shows up. But you can relax. Place looks fine. I didn't see any tracks or anything, but we've only been home about twenty minutes. I was just calling to let you know we were here and not on a ship before I checked on the animals."

"Be careful."

"Unlike you, I always am."

Derek signaled him and mouthed, "Invite them over."

"Hey, you and Mom want to head here?"

"Aren't you the one who just told me the roads were shit?"

"You just said your vehicle could handle it."

"It did, but it was dicey," she admitted.

"We were just about to head over on some sleds. They're two-seaters, so we could bring you back."

"Ha, can you imagine Mom riding a snowmobile?" Selene giggled.

Mom must have been listening because she shouted, "I'll have you know I used to ride a lot as a teen."

"Back when the sleds were drawn by horses," Selene huffed.

"Brat!"

Ares smiled at the banter. "We should be there within the hour."

"I'll check the animals and get our gear together while we wait. I assume there's a rack for us to strap an overnight bag."

"Yes, so long as you don't overpack."

"Just because I had to sit on my suitcase to zip it doesn't mean I overpack."

"Uh, yeah it does."

Selene laughed. "See you in a bit."

He hung up and glanced at Derek. "You heard all that."

"I heard enough. We're bringing home your mom and sis. You go warn Grams while I finish getting our rides ready."

Ares popped inside the warm kitchen to see Athena relaxing with a cup of tea, Grams sitting beside her directing with a wooden spoon. Charly hovered by

Greta, who stood on a step stool carefully measuring some flour.

"Hey, Grams, hope it's okay if Selene and Mom are going to join us."

"What happened to their cruise?" Athena exclaimed.

"Flight got cancelled."

"And they didn't call? That rat." Athena's gaze narrowed. "I specifically texted Selene to see if she and Mom made it okay and she replied with a thumbs-up."

"Apparently she didn't want us worrying."

Athena scowled.

Grams tapped her cup with her spoon. "No frowning. You'll make the baby sour."

Athena glared at her instead.

Grams smiled serenely. "Of course, Bea and Selene are welcome. Ahoy, sous chef Greta. We have two more guests coming." To which the child barked, "Two more mini pie plates, stat."

"Yes, chef," Charly muttered with a roll of her eyes.

"Are you still heading out?" Athena asked, noticing his gear.

"Yeah. We're going to bring them back by sled since the roads are crap."

"And the farm..." Athena didn't say more, but he understood.

"Fine. No sign of trouble."

Not yet.

The ride over proved exhilarating. The sky, while

heavy with clouds, remained clear, although the snow packed nicely as they rode, leaving a trail they could follow back. Since they mostly rode through empty fields and alongside snow-covered roads, they didn't see many people out about, just a few snowmobilers like them. As they headed into the last copse of trees before the farm, they noticed a group of three riders clustered, stopped most likely to get their bearings since the trails weren't officially open.

As they popped out of the trees and sped across the field, the house in sight, Ares noticed the wolf pacing out front. Selene had shifted, which meant something had set her off. She snarled in their direction, but Derek held up a hand and waved as they slowed to a stop a few yards away.

The enemy was here, his wolf announced.

Ares spotted the red and pink speckles in the snow in front of the porch.

Blood.

Probably from the body that lay sprawled and partially buried.

A naked body.

A chilled Ares ripped off his helmet and shouted, "What the fuck happened?"

Selene couldn't reply nor could she shift, not while still upset. She'd always had an issue with strong emotions.

Mom emerged cradling a shotgun. A bruise blossomed on her cheek, and she looked shaken.

"We're okay. Some goons paid us a visit and asked where Charly and Greta were. I told the ringleader I had no idea who they spoke of. He didn't believe me and gave me a smack. When I cried out, Selene came charging out of the barn, and..." Mom glanced at Selene's pacing wolf. "Let's just say she couldn't hold her temper."

"You mentioned goons in the plural. I only see one body."

"The other one bolted once I brought out the gun." Mom's chin lifted. "My lessons with Grams paid off. I nicked it in the ass as they were running off."

Ran off, not drove. The driveway showed no tire tracks other than the ones left by Selene's vehicle. A glance past the carnage showed disturbed snow heading for the forest. Ares already knew the answer but had to ask anyway. "Were they lycanthrope?"

Mom nodded. "They arrived as wolves from the woods. One of them shifted to ask the questions. He's the one over there." She pointed to the body showing tear marks. Selene hadn't messed around with the guy who hurt Mom.

A guy associated with Charly's ex.

When Charly said Barry was a killer, he'd expected the mob kind. But nope, her ex was a werewolf, and even worse, he and Derek had left a trail that would lead right back to Charly and Greta. He couldn't help but recall the snowmobilers he'd seen on the outskirts of their property. Had they passed the fuckers on their way in?

He glanced at Derek. "We gotta get back to the farm."

Selene whined.

"Sorry, sis, but you won't fit on the back while you're a wolf, and there's a body that needs handling before you can go anywhere."

He felt bad leaving his sister and mother to drag it into the woods to be devoured by wildlife; however, urgency fired his blood.

"Mom, call Athena. Tell her to get everyone into the shelter."

"Will try. The cell signal's been spotty. Be careful."

"You, too. Stay in the house, lock the doors, and keep the gun handy in case any come back."

"They'd better not," Mom grumbled. "Any suggestions on where we should drag the body?"

"Dump it in the ravine. The spring melt will float it away from the farm." And the wounds, if still visible when the body was found, would point to a wildlife attack. "Use the ATV to pull it."

With those instructions, he jumped on the sled and revved it back in the direction they'd come. Speeding. Praying. And yes, a little bit scared.

Our mate and pup are in danger.

CHAPTER 14

ATHENA GOT A CALL AND REPLIED. "Hey, Mom, have—" She ceased talking, and her face tightened before she muttered, "Will do. Thanks for the heads-up."

She hung up, and Grams barked, "What's wrong?"

"A few things." Athena eyed Charly. "We need to have a chat." Her gaze drifted to Greta. "Alone."

Grams had an idea. "Sweet thing, we could use some more apples from the cellar. Can you find me a couple fat and juicy ones? They're in the big brown bag."

"On it." Greta scampered to the stairs going down.

Once she was out of sight, Athena hissed, "You should have told us your ex is a werewolf."

Charly's jaw dropped. "I—How—"

"Some of his pack showed up at the farm in wolf

form. Mom says she tried to call sooner, but their cell service has been spotty because of the storm."

"Oh no." Charly slumped into a chair as all strength left her limbs. "Did he hurt them?"

"Selene and Mom are fine, but chances are your ex and some of his pack are on their way here."

"Good." Grams pushed to her feet. "I'll get my rifle. Someone needs to fetch Gramps from the barn."

Athena shook her head. "No fighting. Ares said for us to get into the shelter."

"You ladies can. I'm thinking I'd like a wolf coat for Christmas," Grams' feral reply.

Charly felt faint. They knew. Knew the terrible secret she'd been trying to hide. The one that haunted her and made her think she was crazy. After all, people didn't turn into animals. Only, Barry and his gang did, not that she knew when she'd been with him. He'd only revealed himself her last night at the cabin. It had been the catalyst for her escape.

"Come outside with me," Barry demanded in the doorway to her prison room.

Charlotte knew better than to argue. Her lip remained swollen from her last supposed failure to obey.

She rose, but when Greta would have followed, a silent and pale shadow since their capture, Barry snapped, "Not you. This is for your mother's eyes only."

Charlotte hated leaving Greta alone, but better that than her baby having to see whatever torment Barry had planned.

To her surprise, he had her head outside where all of his gang stood forming a circle around two people kneeling on the ground. The posse parted as Barry arrived.

"I'm about to show you why Greta belongs with me even if she's not showing signs yet."

Showing signs of what? Charlotte wondered but didn't ask, couldn't, not with fear paralyzing her.

The man kneeling on the ground had a bruised and bloodied face. He whimpered, "It was just a wrong turn."

"Sure, it was," drawled Barry.

"The GPS guided us wrong," insisted the woman by his side, her features pale with fear.

"Wrong for you, but you'll make a nice start to our evening," Barry replied. "Right, boys?" A misnomer, which the two women of the gang didn't take offense with.

"Moon's coming," informed Kyle, the youngest of the group. He'd joined the gang with his dad, a big brute of a man who leered at Charlotte when Barry wasn't watching.

"Get ready," Barry stated, which apparently meant strip.

Everyone, man and woman, with the exception of Barry, removed their clothes until they stood naked.

A discomfited Charlotte hugged herself, but it didn't stem the shaking. Why get in the buff? Given a few men sported semi-erections, she feared the worst.

Orgy. Rape. Didn't matter. She wanted no part.

When she would have fled inside the cabin, Barry gripped her arm tight. "Oh no you don't. Time for you to see the truth."

Kyle changed first, one minute a skinny, pimply-faced teen, the next, a mottled brown wolf. One by one, the others swapped skin for fur until only Barry remained dressed, but his eyes had a wild glint to them. His voice emerged in a deeper octave as he barked, "Show my bitch what we do to those who would betray us."

It was beyond savage. Beyond bloody. Beyond horrifying.

The wolves pounced on the couple who'd taken a wrong turn. She closed her eyes at the first scream but couldn't unhear the noises. The growls. The wet munching. The crunching.

The wolves savaged the poor man and his girlfriend, killing them and then desecrating the bodies by tearing them open to chew on the insides.

Charlotte didn't resist when Barry dragged her back inside. As he marched her to her room, he muttered, "Now you understand why Greta belongs with me."

"Greta isn't a werewolf," her faint reply.

"Not yet. I thought my blessing skipped her, but she carries the gene, according to the sample I had tested."

"What sample?" she asked, rather than address the horror she'd just witnessed.

"Turns out there's a way to check if someone inherited lycanthropy. I had Martha volunteer at her

school and collect some spit and hair. Turns out, she does take after me." Martha being the petite blonde who'd hated Charlotte on sight.

"Your test was wrong. She's not a werewolf."

"Not yet. While I've always known what I am, I found out only recently that some who carry the gift don't shift until their teens, meaning I gave up too quick."

"She's nothing like you," her scratchy reply.

"She will be," an ominous statement.

Barry shoved Charlotte into the room, but before he slammed the door shut, he smiled and said, "Count yourself lucky I've decided to let you live. After all, a child needs some siblings."

"No." She recoiled.

The sadistic bastard laughed. "Not tonight. Tonight, the moon calls, and I must answer."

With that, the door slammed shut, and she heard the lock engage.

Greta stared at her wide-eyed, but rather than console her, Charlotte flew to the window in time to see Barry emerge from the house, naked. As he approached his gang huddled over the hunks of meat—the bodies torn to pieces—he changed.

Changed into a wolf and she knew in that moment she had to escape. That night. And disappear.

"Is Greta a lycanthrope?" Athena asked, snapping Charly back to the present.

She shook her head. "No. She's just a little girl."

"Whose father is a werewolf. She might not have changed yet, but she has his genetics, meaning she might eventually shift." Athena had a serious mien.

"What would you even know about it?" Charlotte blurted out.

"Because I'm a werewolf, too," Athena stated.

Charlotte blinked. "You're like Barry?" She took a step away.

"Oh for fuck's sake, I'm not going to suddenly go four-legged and eat you. Your ex and his pack might be psychos who kill, but that's not the norm for our kind."

"How would you know?" It hit Charlotte suddenly. "You know more wolves." The revelations kept happening. "Your sister, Ares, your mom…"

"Ares and Selene, yes. Mom, no. We inherited our lycanthropy from Dad."

Charlotte put her face in her hands. "I can't. This is too much."

"Now's not the time to fall apart," barked Grams.

"Are you a werewolf?" her sarcastic reply.

"No, but my grandbaby will most likely be, and I'm fine with it."

Charlotte glanced at Grams. "But they're wolves."

"So what? Will you love Greta any less when she starts to change?"

"Of course not. I probably won't even fight when she tries to eat me." Her lips turned down.

Athena snorted. "For god's sake, no one's eating

you, unless it's my brother, and that will be the kind of eating you like, not the OMG-I'm-dying kind."

A hot blush flushed Charlotte's cheeks.

"In case you hadn't noticed, Ares and the others aren't ravening beasts."

"Maybe not in their human shape," Charlotte pointed out.

Athena rolled her eyes. "Even as wolves, we don't lose control and kill wantonly."

"But you do kill."

"I hunt, yes, rabbits and other small creatures. It is, after all, in our nature. But we don't go after humans unless they're trying to harm us."

Slightly reassuring. But still… "I can't believe my boyfriend pees on trees." Charlotte tried to wrap her head around the fact the man she'd touched, the man she was falling for, had a hairy side.

Grams slapped her hand on the table. "While we're yapping, time is passing. Athena, go fetch Gramps. He's out in the barn with the horses. We'll meet you in the shelter."

"On it." Athena threw on some boots and a plaid jacket by the door before heading out.

Grams spoke gently. "This changes nothing. Ares is still the same man you fell in love with."

"I don't love him," a quick retort, but not entirely true. Charlotte had been falling for him. Hard. Only to discover that, once more, she hadn't spotted the monster inside the man.

"Don't you lie to me, girl. You're head over heels for him and him with you. He's a good man. His whole family is. Do you think I'd let my grandson be with Athena if they weren't? Just because you met one bad werewolf doesn't mean they're all shitheads."

Conversation ceased as Greta appeared, holding several apples. "Found them!" she chirped.

"Fantastic. Put them on the counter. We're going to have an adventure," Grams stated softly. "In my special room under the house."

"With Mama?" Greta glanced at Charlotte.

"Yes, with your mama. Shall we go check it out?"

Grams rose and held out her hand. Greta took it, and things were fine as they went down into the cellar. Remained fine until Greta realized what Grams meant by special room.

"There's no windows," Greta remarked, peeking inside the shelter.

"To keep us safe," Gram murmured.

Greta glanced at the door, thick metal, with bars that would slide across to keep it shut. Her daughter's face shifted to her stubborn look, and she shook her head. "No. No special room. Won't go back." Greta bolted away from the bunker and up the stairs.

"Greta, come back!" Only her child didn't reply, and it hit Charlotte that Greta thought they'd be imprisoned again.

Grams grumbled. "We'd better go find her."

"Sorry. I didn't realize the bunker would trigger

her memories of when her father had us captive. We spoke about it a little when we escaped, but given her age, it seemed easier to just let her forget."

"Kids never forget anything. Like elephants they are," Grams muttered.

They reached the kitchen. No Greta.

"I'll search this floor; you check upstairs," Grams suggested.

Charlotte started with the room Greta had used. Looked in the closet, under the bed, all the while calling her.

No reply. No sign of her daughter.

She checked her room next, then the one Derek and Athena shared, all the while aware they wasted time.

She'd just about given up, ready to join Grams in her search downstairs, when she peeked in the bathroom. Not many places to hide, but the shower curtain was drawn over the tub.

Charlotte crouched before pulling it back, the rings holding the plastic sheet rattling.

Greta sat huddled in the tub, hugging her knees. "Not going. No wanna be locked in a room."

"Oh, munchkin, the bunker in the basement is different. It's to protect us."

"From the bad man?" Greta asked in a little voice. She'd never called Barry dad, no matter how many times he told her he was her father.

Charlotte nodded.

"Is he coming?"

She didn't want to lie. "He might be."

Greta whimpered, and Charlotte's heart broke.

"I won't let him hurt you."

"He hurt my mama," she whispered.

Charlotte couldn't deny the claim. She'd tried to fight, but Barry had the strength and the mean streak to counter. But she knew a man who wouldn't be daunted. A man her daughter admired. "Ares is on his way back. He'll keep us safe."

"I don't want the bad man to hurt Ares."

"Oh please," Charlotte exclaimed. "Ares is a hero. The bad man can't hurt him." Words that struck a chord. The man she'd grown to care for wasn't an ugly bully. He didn't mistreat her. Didn't make her afraid. But would that change when he turned into his wolf?

"Ares is a hero," Greta repeated. "He won't let the bad man take me," Greta stated with confidence, standing up in the tub. Charlotte held her hand as they exited the bathroom and headed downstairs.

Before she could lead Greta to the bunker, a rumbling sound from outdoors drew their attention.

"Ares is back!" Greta chirped, yanking free and racing for the door.

It seemed too soon for him to have returned. An ugly feeling knotted Charlotte's stomach, and she bolted to catch Greta.

Too late.

She emerged to find her daughter in none other

than Barry's grip. The bastard had arrived on a brand-new-looking snowmobile, and he didn't come alone. She recognized Hughey, Ivan, and Amir.

At the sight of Charlotte, Barry smirked. "Did you really think I wouldn't find you?"

Chk-chk. A shotgun armed behind Charlotte, and Grams snarled, "Unhand the child."

"Or what?" Barry drawled as he tucked Greta to his chest. "Gonna shoot me?"

Grams uttered a low growl, making Charlotte wonder if she told the truth about not being a werewolf.

"I didn't think so." Barry laughed. "Drop the gun." When Grams hesitated, the bastard tightened his hold, and Greta squeaked.

Grams set the gun down.

"Don't hurt her," Charlotte pleaded.

"The pup will be fine, but as for the rest of you..." He offered a nasty smile. "Get inside and don't try anything, or I might decide fatherhood isn't my thing after all."

Grams hobbled in first, murmuring softly, "Don't mention Athena or Gramps. All is not lost yet."

Funny, because it sure felt as if it were. Charlotte saw no way out of this. The best she could hope for was Barry would leave and not harm anyone. But that would leave Greta in his clutches. Better Charlotte die trying to save her.

Barry herded them into the living room, a wide-eyed, lip-trembling Greta still tight to his chest. Amir stood behind him, arms crossed.

"You had a lot of nerve leaving," Barry stated. "You made me look bad in front of the boys."

"Ah yes because kidnapping and terrorizing a child is a much better look," Charlotte muttered.

"Only because you wouldn't cooperate. You could have just done as you were told like a proper bitch, but, no, you chose instead to make me chase you."

"How did you find me?" she asked.

"I had Martha scouring social media. Didn't actually think you'd be dumb enough to have your face on camera."

Charlotte wanted to curse. If only she'd not taken Greta to that damned Christmas market.

"Now you're probably wondering how I found you here. It was actually easier than expected. See, after I chatted with your boyfriend I found out he was the same guy you left with from your place. Fucker lied to me, and when I returned, he was gone. So we decided to stake out his farm. Stole some sleds and parked ourselves in the woods waiting, and it paid off. He arrived by snowmobile and left us a clear path right back to you."

"Ares is coming," Greta stated.

"I'm counting on that. Wonder if he'll like the surprise I left him."

Charlotte's heart stopped. "What did you do?"

"Made sure we wouldn't be interrupted. We have

unfinished business, Charlotte. Can't exactly have you roaming around flapping your lips about what you think you know."

"I didn't tell anyone," she huffed.

"The first smart thing you did. However, here's the problem. I gave you a chance, and you betrayed me. You can't be trusted, and there's only one solution to that dilemma."

No need to say it. He was going to kill her.

A tremble took hold of Charlotte's limbs, and her lips were numb as she said, "Please don't do anything in front of Greta." She might not be able to save herself, but she wanted to prevent Greta from seeing it.

"Begging is a nice look for you, but no can do. The pup needs to understand who's the alpha and what happens to those who cross me." Barry held Greta out to Amir. "Hold her while I handle the bitch myself."

The man grabbed a squirming Greta. "No. No. Leave Mama alone. Nooo—grrrrr."

Everyone went still as the child suddenly turned into a little wolf. Amir dropped her, and Greta, the wolf puppy, wiggled free of her clothes and crouched on four paws on the floor, snarling, her bristly hackles rising in spikes along her spine.

A nasty smile spread across Barry's face. "Well, I'll be. Guess we won't need to wait until she's a teen after all." He reached for Greta, who snapped and snarled.

"None of that, you brat," he commanded in a cold tone.

He lunged for Greta again and managed to get her by the scruff and lift her.

Greta whimpered, and Grams made a low sound.

Oddly, the tree they'd decorated the night before rattled, the branches shaking. No one seemed to notice but Charlotte. No one saw the little nose that peeked, but everyone heard Barry's bellow when the tree toppled against him, and the squirrel leaped from a branch to his head. The rodent, with a white streak on its head, dug in its claws and hung on.

A startled Barry dropped Greta, who hit the floor with a thump and sat there dazed.

A very pissed Barry wildly shook his head, and when the squirrel wouldn't let go, he reached for it. Missed it by an inch, as the critter leaped and landed on a chair from which it sprang past a gaping Amir, heading for freedom through the still open front door.

Seeing a chance for Greta, Charlotte screamed, "Run, munchkin!"

The little wolf, utterly panicked, bolted through Amir's legs outside into the coming storm.

Her departure left Charlotte and Grams alone to face a very angry Barry, who had scratches on his face and a scowl on his lips.

"Get the girl while I handle these bitches," Barry ordered.

Amir left, and Barry sneered in their direction. "Time to give you my version of a gift for the holidays. Eternal rest. In pieces, you old bat." He cackled.

Grams wasn't in the mood to be threatened. "Old? Come here and let's see who's old now that you ain't using a child as a meat shield anymore, asshole."

Perhaps Grams could have wrestled a man as big as Barry. Only he didn't stay a man.

A wolf exploded from the clothes, big and scary looking.

Not to Grams, who smacked her lips and said, "You'll make a mighty fine coat."

Charlotte agreed, but that would require them killing the wolf when it seemed more likely they'd get torn to pieces.

Ares, where are you?

Because she could really use a hero right about now.

CHAPTER 15

THE SNOWMOBILES THREATENED TO overheat as Ares and Derek pushed the machines to their limits retracing their path. Their trek started out easy, but as the sky darkened, visibility worsened. Swirling snow began to obscure their route, forcing them to slow at certain junctions to ensure they went in the right direction. Ares hated the delay, especially since when they first began racing to the farm, they couldn't help but notice the tracks overlaying and running parallel to the ones created on their way over.

Once more he couldn't help but remember that group of sleds on the other side of his property. They had to have seen them go by. Had that been Barry and his pack? It killed to know he might have driven right by them and given them a way to backtrack.

The only thing that kept him somewhat calm was

knowing the bunker would keep them safe—as long as they got inside before trouble arrived.

When Derek slowed down, it forced Ares to ease off the gas as well. Before he could shout and ask what was wrong, he saw the problem through the shifting snow. A sled parked across the path, and no one sitting on it.

Derek rolled up slowly and pointed. Two piles of clothes lay draped on the seat. It appeared they'd found part of Barry's pack.

Danger.

The warning had Ares throwing himself off his sled to the side and landing in the snow. Better a helmeted face plant though snow than the snapping jaws of the wolf that suddenly attacked.

He rolled and bounced to his feet, cursing the fact he wore too many layers. His own beast could have easily taken the one he faced, but he was more likely to get bound up in his borrowed snowsuit than become deadly.

The wolf stood on the seat of his machine and snarled.

Ares flipped up his visor and snarled back, which caused some surprise.

"That's right, you fucking mongrel. You're not the only one with teeth around here."

The wolf lunged, leaping for him, and Ares let the beast hit him, mostly so he could grab it by the forelegs and flip it. The wolf went sailing and yelped as it slammed into a tree.

Bang.

A quick glance over his shoulder showed Derek had the rifle, and while he'd managed to get off a shot, he missed, and the second wolf converged on him too quickly to fire again. He swung the gun like a club, knocking it in the head, but that didn't stop it from pouncing and taking Derek to the ground.

His friend would have to hold on for help, as Ares had his wolf to deal with. The shaggy mongrel shook its head and bared its teeth but showed more caution, as it prowled and tried to circle.

"I don't have time for this," Ares muttered. He grabbed a branch and snapped it free. Not the greatest weapon, but he had nothing else. It hadn't occurred to him they'd have trouble on the trail. He should have grabbed the rifle he kept locked in the house or the crossbow in the shed.

The wolf came at a run. Only a few paces separated them. As it leaped, Ares crouched and, as the beast reached the point over his head, thrust upward. The stick didn't penetrate far, but the wolf squealed.

Blood dripped from the wolf's wound even before it landed. Bad idea for the mongrel as it shoved the makeshift stake deeper. The wolf whimpered, deadly injured, and it knew it.

One down. He went to help Derek, who held the rifle

sideways with a wolf latched to the barrel. Ares would have had to go out of his way for another stick, precious seconds he didn't have, so he ran instead at the wolf and leaped.

He landed boots first on its spine with enough force something cracked, and the beast dropped. But it didn't die. It tried to crawl away, using its front paws to pull its paralyzed hindquarters.

"Where do you think you're going?" Ares snarled as he planted himself in front of the wolf.

The wounded wolf changed into a bleeding man, who blubbered, "Don't kill me."

"Give me one good reason I shouldn't."

"I didn't want to do this. Barry made us."

"Where is the fucker?" he asked, glancing at the other body. The one he'd stabbed breathed still, but shallowly. Almost dead.

"He's gone to get his kid."

Ares whipped his head around sharply. "Where?"

"Dunno. We was just following this trail when he waved us off and told us to stop anyone that came through."

"How far ahead is he?" Couldn't be that far since they'd not been long at the farm.

"I don't know. I'm cold." The guy shivered, but Ares honestly didn't care.

Derek, however, had some words for him. "So, here's the deal. You made a very poor life choice in following this Barry fucker, but that doesn't mean you can't turn your life around. You're going to get on that sled and leave. And by leave, I mean fuck off to wherever you came from because if I ever see you poking your nose in this area again, I will feed you to my woodchipper and fertilize our garden with your shredded remains. Do I make myself clear?"

"How am I supposed to ride? My legs don't work," chattered the man.

"Not my problem. You chose this."

Ares pursed his lips. "Are you sure we shouldn't just save ourselves the trouble and kill him now?"

"He's young enough that if he survives, he can still repent and mend his ways."

"He'd better..." Ares growled.

They didn't wait to see if the guy managed to get going. They hopped their sleds and sped away, racing almost blindly on the trail they'd forged, the visibility getting worse and worse as the next storm rolled in early.

By the time they hit the marker indicating they'd reached the outskirts of the farm, snowflakes came down thick and fast.

They didn't slow down and soon, despite the storm, could see the glowing lights of the house... and a few snowmobiles parked out front.

Ares no sooner cut his engine than Charlotte, along with Grams and Gramps, were on the porch, the latter holding guns.

Charlotte looked frantic.

She wasn't the only one.

"Where's Athena?" Derek hollered as he tore off his helmet.

"She went after the thugs that tried to kidnap Greta," Grams announced with a scowl.

"She did what? Is she insane?" Derek yelled.

"We told her to wait for you boys, but given the little one took off with those assholes hot on her tail, Athena decided to follow in her wolf form. Good thing she was agitated enough to shift."

"Wait a second. Are you saying Greta's out there in this storm?" Ares couldn't help his shock—and fear. The woods could be dangerous in fair conditions, but in this type of weather, and with parts of the forest booby-trapped, it could turn deadly, especially for a small child.

"I wanted to follow, but Athena told me to stay back." Charlotte's voice cracked. "Said she was better equipped to find her."

"I'm going after them." Ares tossed his helmet to the snowmobile seat.

"Before you go haring off too, there's something you need to know." Charlotte swallowed hard before whispering, "Greta turned into a wolf."

"What?" Ares said dumbly, but then reality hit. If Barry was a lycanthrope, then it made sense Greta would be too.

Charlotte wrung her hands. "I never believed she was one until today. When Barry tried to hurt me, Greta changed. I told her to run, but he went after her." Her lips quavered as she whispered, "You have to find her. She's so tiny. Just a baby still."

"I'll bring her back."

We will find her and destroy those that would harm the pup.

"They don't have much of a head start," Grams stated. "It's been less than ten minutes since the little one bolted."

An eternity in a storm that rapidly erased tracks and scents.

He glanced at Derek. "I expect you're coming too. Be sure to bring a gun, along with a pack of warm gear for Greta and Athena."

"You aren't carrying anything?"

"Kind of hard since I'm going on four feet."

He heard Charlotte's sharp inhalation. "So it's true?"

Ares feared looking at her and seeing the condemnation. He now understood her terror of her ex. Would she be scared of him too? "Yeah. I'm a lycan but..." He dared to glance at her. "Nothing like that fucker."

"I believe you," her faint reply. "Can you find Greta?"

"I won't come back without her," he swore. "Now if y'all don't mind, I am going to get naked."

He could have hidden to change. After all, he'd been concealing this side of himself his whole life from everyone but his immediate family. But these people were family now too, and Charlotte needed to see his wolf wasn't something to be feared. He wanted—make that needed—her to accept him as he was.

So behave, he warned his other half as his fingers made quick work of his clothing.

She shall see and admire my prowess, his conceited wolf declared.

Or she'd scream.

Hopefully, the former.

The biting wind stung the skin and whipped it with snow, a discomfort that lasted only seconds as he willed his beast to come forth. It didn't take much coaxing. Unlike his sisters, Ares had always had excellent control when it came to shifting. He could even fight the lure of moonlight—he just usually chose not to.

He hit the ground on four paws and gave himself a shake to loosen his fur. More a passenger than the driver in this shape, but he trusted in his beast.

Find the pup.

With one last glance at Charlotte, who stared wide-eyed but thankfully not cringing, he set off.

He trotted quickly, noting the tracks filling rapidly with snow. Paw prints, large male ones, alongside a smaller set that belonged to Athena, but it was the sight of the tiny imprints that jarred most.

Princess was a wolf like him. No wonder they'd established a bond so quickly.

Told you: Pup.

Ares hadn't taken his beast literally.

Couldn't you smell it?

No. Greta seemed like a normal child. Then again, all lycanthropes passed as human on the outside. It took analyzing their DNA at a deeper level to spot the difference.

As Ares entered the woods, the whipping snow diminished, but so did visibility. Good thing he didn't need his eyes to track. His nose only had to occasionally dip, the recent lingering scents guiding his steps. A distant bark perked his ears. Barry had three others with him. Four against one. Ares liked the odds. For himself at least. Athena, while tough, was no match for four full-grown males.

When he heard snarling up ahead, his pace quickened. A sharp-pitched yip raised his hackles.

The pup is in danger.

No shit. He brushed past some snowy bushes to see a fight happening. Athena held the high ground, standing atop a large rock, her white fur blending against the snowy backdrop. She appeared uninjured, no red streaking her flanks, and her eyes blazed with anger. Standing behind her, shivering and yet standing brave, a little wolf.

Princess.

The pup.

Facing off against them, four mangy curs. The biggest one snarled and barked at Athena, but each time he went to approach the rock, she swung her head low and snapped her teeth.

She's fierce. His wolf approved.

So are we.

Ares gave no warning, and yet one of the wolves heard him coming and turned his head just as Ares soared. The russet wolf could do nothing to stop Ares from slamming into his side, tumbling them both in a tangle of limbs. Jaws clacked as they strove to dominate. Not really much of a contest because Ares was the bigger wolf—meaner, too, with his princess threatened.

He clamped his teeth around a neck and squeezed, kept crunching even as bones snapped, kept applying pressure until the body went limp. Not exactly the kind of thing he wanted princess to see, but at least there was little blood.

Before he'd fully unlatched, another wolf came barking at him. Ares avoided getting bitten only narrowly. This wolf was older and wilier. Obviously experienced in fighting, judging by the scars bisecting its fur. They rolled in the snow as each sought to get a killing hold. A sharp yip was the only warning he got before another of the mongrels latched onto his leg. The pain proved fleeting, as Athena slammed into the brute, knocking him free.

While Ares dealt with his pair, the biggest wolf lunged at Athena, grabbing her fur with his teeth and yanking hard enough his sister yelped.

Athena!

How dare he injure our sibling.

Ares uttered a mighty howl and kicked his paw out at the wolf still nagging him. The surprise move, which didn't involve teeth, resulted in a claw raking across the other beast's eye. It howled in pain and recoiled, shaking its head. It wasn't interested in fighting anymore, but his companion hadn't learned its lesson yet. The brindled wolf came at Ares, jaw dripping drool, rabid with bloodlust. It made him clumsy. Ares moved to the side as it lunged and whipped his head around to grab it by the neck, hard enough the neck snapped. The body went limp, leaving Ares free to handle the big brute going after Athena.

He hung his head low and snarled, drawing the wolf's attention away from his sister. Athena moved to the left, trapping the brute between them.

Some might say, not fair, two against one, but fairness didn't exist in the lycanthrope world. It especially didn't exist for a piece of shit who abused women and terrorized children.

As if synchronized, they both lunged at Barry—had to be him, as the others lacked the alpha vibe. The brute swung his head left and right, snapping his teeth, snarling, but couldn't stop the attack. Athena sank her teeth into his haunch, possibly severing a tendon, seeing as how the leg went limp. Ares aimed for the neck but missed and got a mouthful of fur.

Barry realized he was outmatched and shook

himself free before running away, slowly, his injured leg dragging. Ares could have let him go, but so long as the fucker breathed, he'd pose a danger to Charly and Greta. To his whole family.

Ares uttered a sharp bark.

Stay with the pup, the command for his sister before Ares went after Barry. Unlike the injured enemy, he remained sleek and fast. The woods he navigated might have been unfamiliar, but the scents were ones he'd grown up with. Fir tree. Pine. On an open stretch, where Barry tried to pick up some speed, he spotted a depression in the fresh fallen snow and remembered a conversation he'd had with Derek a while back.

"Just so you know, if you ever decide to wolf out on the property, keep in mind Grams and Gramps have set traps in the woods. Stick to the main paths to avoid them."

"What kind of traps?" he'd asked.

"Metal jaws, snares, even some pits. You should see the bear they found in one last year."

The recollection slowed his steps, but Barry didn't slow. He ran over the sunken spot.

Which dropped, taking the wolf with it!

Ares cautiously approached the pit, making sure to steer clear of the edge but still peeking over the side to see.

A wolf's body, its head bent at an unnatural angle, lay at the bottom, the death abrupt. Final.

The terror the man caused, over.

Good.

Even better, Barry hadn't had time to shift, meaning he'd remain a wolf, so no body to get rid of.

With that threat handled, Ares trotted back for his sister and Greta. The wolf he'd blinded had fled, no longer interested in a fight he couldn't win. Ares debated going after him, but a distant yelp and sharp howl, which ended abruptly, made him think it wouldn't be necessary. *Thank you, Grams and Gramps, for being paranoid.*

Athena stood in front of the rock, shielding Greta's body with her own.

Ares trotted close and slunk down so as to not loom over the little pup.

Big eyes regarded him, and his princess uttered a small whining noise. He edged closer and huffed.

Don't be afraid.

Despite it being her first shift, she understood he meant no harm and crept out from behind Athena until she could rub noses with him.

Everything will be all right.

He'd take care of his little princess. His little wolf.

Greta leaned against him and sighed. Athena uttered a noise and looked in the direction of the farm.

Head back?

He bobbed his head.

In a minute. The little one needed comforting.

He nosed her over, checking to make sure she'd not suffered. No blood and she didn't flinch, so most likely no bruising either. She'd stopped shaking and seemed curious about her new shape, holding out her paws to examine. Her tail flicked, and her head turned and kept turning as she spun in a circle trying to catch it.

He chuffed in amusement.

Greta plopped on her furry butt, and her tongue lolled.

Everything will be just fine.

The pup's little body stiffened, but he didn't stress, even as they heard the huff of someone breathing hard and the crunch of snow. He knew who came.

Our mate.

The little pup leaned against him shivering, not in cold, he suspected, but fear. Fear of what her mother might say or think. He nuzzled her to show she would always be welcome with him. Athena matched his actions on the other side. Flanking the little pup, they waited for Charlotte and Derek to step into view, the flashlights they held to pierce the storm's darkness wavering as they bobbed with their movement. Once the lights steadied, it spotlighted the trio of wolves.

He held his head high and with pride. He refused to cower and hide.

The question being, would Charly accept him as he was?

CHAPTER 16

THE MOMENT ARES DISAPPEARED INTO THE forest looking for Greta, Charlotte wanted to follow. Grams sensed it, so while she outfitted Derek with a bag full of supplies—blankets, socks, flashlights, matches, even food and water—she also layered Charlotte in one of Gramps' winter coats and long johns. Footwear proved tricky, as her feet were smaller than Athena's but larger than Grams'. They had to stuff the toes of Athena's boots to keep them on. The hat and mittens fit fine.

Bundled and feeling like the Michelin Man, she'd trailed after Derek as he hiked quickly into the woods, following the fading tracks Ares left behind. The snow still came down thick, but the wind had died down, so at least it didn't sting the face. Visibility remained poor, however, and once they entered the forest, it turned dark, despite it being midafternoon.

As they walked—and Charlotte huffed from the exertion of clomping in oversized gear—she found herself asking, "What's it like being in a relationship with a werewolf?"

Derek took a second to reply. "Depends on what you mean. Is Athena different from other women I dated? Yes, it's part of what attracted me to her. But even if she hadn't been a wolf, I think we would have meshed because it's her personality I love."

"You're not afraid she'll hurt you when she..." Charlotte paused for lack of a word. "Changes?"

"Werewolves, or lycans as they prefer to be called, aren't savage beasts."

"Barry is."

"But that's not because of his genetics. He's an asshole in general."

"How did you find out about her? I honestly never suspected Barry had another side to him, and we dated for just over a year."

"There are subtle indications. Athena's got an excellent sense of smell and insane hearing. She has this thing when she's excited; her foot will start tapping. And she's always chasing stuff around the yard."

"I haven't noticed any of those things with Ares."

"Ares does a better job of keeping his wolf side in check."

"Will your baby be a wolf?"

"Most likely. And I kind of hope so, even as it scares me."

She glanced at him. "Scares you?"

"Not because I'm worried my child will hurt me, but because others might hurt her." He paused before saying, "When I met Athena, she'd just escaped a doctor who wanted to out her to the world. Turn her into a celebrity freak. He did awful things to her."

"Oh shit," Charlotte whispered, thinking of Greta.

"He's gone now. However, we're always conscious of the fact someone else might come looking, might realize there's something different about Athena and her family."

"I never suspected Greta was like her father." She'd seemed completely normal, AKA human.

"Neither did Ares or Athena. It's not something you can see or smell."

They kept trudging, until Derek cursed. "Fuck, I can't see the tracks anymore." He pulled out his flashlight, they both did, and shone them around. However, the falling snow had obscured the paw prints they'd been following.

"Should we call for them?"

Derek pursed his lips. "I don't want to distract if they're fighting or hiding."

Fighting? It made sense. For some reason as they'd walked, she'd forgotten Barry and his goons also chased Greta. She'd been more intent on finding her daughter.

Cheep.

A chirp drew their gaze to a squirrel sitting on a

branch. A squirrel with a white tuft on its head, kind of like the one that leapt from the tree to frazzle Barry.

"This is going to sound strange, but I think I recognize him," she murmured. "Pretty sure that's the same squirrel that was in the tree Ares brought over." The white tuft on its head was quite distinctive.

Derek chuckled. "Well, I'll be damned. Skippy must have been hiding in it."

"Skippy?"

"Squirrel that's been taunting Ares for the past few years. Seems to think the whole tree farm is his domain and gives my boy shit every time he has to cut one down."

The squirrel chattered before leaping to a branch on a tree slightly ahead and to their left. It glanced back at them and chirped some more.

"Is it just me, or does he want us to follow him?" Derek asked.

Follow a squirrel? Couldn't be any stranger than her kid being a werewolf.

Hence, they plodded in the direction the squirrel led, with Derek watching the trees intently, enough she asked, "What are you looking for?"

"Trap markers."

"Er, what?"

"Grams and Gramps don't like intruders, and so they have the forest kind of booby-trapped."

Charlotte froze in place. "Isn't that dangerous?"

"Only if you don't know what to look for." He

pointed to a tree with a nick in its bark. "That means there's a snare, so keep to the left."

She eyed the spot suspiciously as they passed. "How many of them are there?"

"Not as many as there used to be. Gramps has been slowly dismantling them because of Athena. Wants her to have a safe place to run when the full moon comes. So far, he's disarmed the northern and western parts of our property. But this southern section still has a few."

And her child and Ares and Athena were out here with them!

The squirrel kept them in sight, leaping from branch to branch until it stopped and chattered.

"I think we're just about there. We should turn off our flashlights until we know what's happening," Derek suggested. They crept forward, her heart racing, her breath huffing and steaming. They paused to listen but heard nothing. Saw even less.

Derek finally whispered, "Doesn't sound like there's anyone there."

"What do you mean?" Had the squirrel led them wrong?

Derek flipped on his light and forged ahead with her huffing to keep up with her own bobbing light.

When they emerged into a small clearing, it took a moment for their flashlights to steady enough to see.

In the glare, they saw them, three wolves, the two larger beasts keeping the little one tucked between them. A little pup that stared at her with big eyes.

Until that moment, Charlotte had not been sure how she'd react. Her child was a lycanthrope. A werewolf. A beast that liked to hunt—and kill. An anomaly that would be in danger if the wrong people—aka the government—ever found out.

But the little wolf was also Greta. Her sweet baby girl who'd been a blessing and a joy. Seeing her, tiny body shaking, eyes big and sad with trepidation, Charlotte realized she was still the same baby she'd always loved.

"Munchkin!" She dropped to her knees and held out her arms, and the little wolf barreled across the snow and slammed into her.

Charlotte laughed as she fell on her butt in the snow with Greta atop her, tail wagging, body wiggling, tongue licking the salty tears from her chapped cheeks. She'd not even realized she'd begun crying.

"Goodness, you're a squirmy little puppy. Does this mean you're going to stop asking for a dog?" she quipped.

The wolf puppy suddenly transformed into a very naked child, who replied, "I'd rather have a squirrel."

"Of course, you would." Charlotte laughed.

"Here, put this on." Derek had the pack open and pulled forth some clothes. Charlotte dressed her child, keeping her focus on Greta rather than the other two wolves, one of them quite large.

Sweater, pants, socks, boots, coat, hat, mitts. Soon

Greta was dressed and grimacing. "It's so much harder to move in this. I should have stayed a wolf."

Derek had left her side to deal with Athena, who also transformed to get dressed, leaving only Ares in wolf shape. He sported thick dark fur, unlike his sister's snowy coat and Greta's grayish one, his size more on par with a pony than a dog, which made sense given his weight as a man. He eyed her warily. With reason. He knew how she felt about Barry—and why. Barry had been a sadistic killer. A bully. A fraud who'd hidden his dark side.

But Ares wasn't anything like him.

Ares had been nothing but kind to her. Had taken care of them. Had charged into danger to save her child.

It took less nerve than expected to approach him. To reach out and stroke the hair on his head.

"Scratch him behind his ears if you wanna get his leg thumping," Athena stated.

With that advice, she did, and not only his leg went nuts, but his tail did, too. Greta joined her, murmuring, "Ares saved me, Mama. Him and Athena."

"I know. I owe them my deepest gratitude."

Greta hugged the giant wolf. "He's a hero. Wish he was my dada."

Speaking of whom, while Charlotte spotted some red splotches in the snow, and two dead wolves, neither appeared to be Barry.

She glanced at Athena and mouthed, *Where's Barry?*

Athena's lips moved. *Dead.*

Good. At least she wouldn't have to worry about him coming after Greta anymore. As for the fall-out if his body were discovered... She'd deal with it if and when it happened. Was it wrong to feel relief her child's father had perished? Probably, but she honestly didn't care, not after what he'd done.

A furry head nudged her hand, and the expression in Ares' eyes spoke to her. *You're safe.*

For the first time in a while, she no longer had to run or hide.

"Let's head back to the house," Derek stated. "Sorry, bro, but the pack didn't have room for more stuff, so you'll have to four-leg it."

Ares took the lead, trotting with his tail high, unerring in his path but also accommodating. While he could move quickly, a stumping Greta and Charlotte couldn't. By the time they emerged from the forest, the thick falling snow had tapered to a light sprinkle. Lanterns had been lit and placed outside the house, giving them a warm welcome. Although the heat inside proved to be the best thing of all.

Charlotte hadn't realized just how cold she was until she began to thaw. She took off the layers and gratefully cradled the cup of hot cocoa with a shot of something that warmed the belly.

Grams had Greta wrapped in a big blanket by the

woodstove with a cup of something steamy. Athena rolled her eyes as Derek quietly harangued her. But where was Ares?

She went into the hall to see him slipping up the stairs, a blanket around his hips.

"Why are you sneaking off?"

He glanced at her. "Just getting some clothes."

"Thank you for what you did."

"As if I'd let anyone hurt princess."

"Did you know about..." She couldn't quite say it.

He shook his head. "My wolf did, but I didn't clue in what it was telling me."

"Guess that explains why you bonded so quickly."

His lips quirked. "You don't think it was my charm and good looks?"

She laughed. "Oh, that most definitely helped."

"Are you okay?" he asked in a more serious tone.

"Surprisingly, I think I am."

"And if I say she might shift again tomorrow night on the full moon..."

She blinked. "I forgot it was coming. You think she'll do it again so soon?"

He shrugged. "Maybe. Some shift on the full moon from birth. Some don't grow into it until their teens."

"But she didn't have a moon today and still changed. All of you did."

"It's possible, but not everyone can do it. Most

require strong emotions. Like Selene, she shifts when she's mad. Athena really has to make an effort."

"Not you?"

"Not me."

"Will you teach Greta about being a lycanthrope?" She used the new unfamiliar term so as to not insult.

"It would be my pleasure."

"And me? Will you also show me how to support her?" She paused before softly adding, "And you?"

He forgot about getting dressed as he came back down the few steps to stand in front of her and murmur, "It would be my utmost pleasure."

She gazed at him. "I'm really happy you stalked me, Ares McMurray." She said it before she could lose her nerve.

"Me too, Charly."

He kissed her, a soft sweet and tender kiss interrupted by a child, who hollered, "Mama, Grams is roasting hotdogs in the fireplace. Come see!"

Ares sighed. "Guess I'd better get used to being cock-blocked."

She stroked his cheek. "Only until she goes to bed."

Which turned out to not be as early as expected because a child on Christmas Eve had too much hyper energy, not to mention leftover excitement from surviving a day fraught with danger.

Eventually, Greta went to bed—after giving everyone a hug and kiss.

But Charlotte couldn't quite sneak off with Ares yet. The flurry to wrap the presents—with help—and get them under the tree happened next. Stockings were stuffed. The plate of cookies devoured along with the milk.

Eventually, good nights were said, and as Ares took her hand to lead her upstairs, her heart fluttered. For some reason it felt different this time; she couldn't have said why. It took his soft smile for it to hit her.

There was nothing standing between her and Ares. No secrets. No more being chased by her past. They could be together.

As the door closed behind them, he held her hands and murmured, "Why are you trembling? Are you afraid of me?"

She shook her head and then said what was in her heart. "On the contrary, I think I love you."

CHAPTER 17

Ares almost died hearing her soft admission and then took so long to reply that her head ducked and she whispered, "I'm sorry. I shouldn't have said it. It's too soon."

He crushed her to him. "Don't you dare take it back. You took me by surprise because I expected you to take longer to realize it."

"You knew I'd fallen for you?"

"Can't blame you, because I'm awesome, but if it helps, I fell in love first. From the moment we met, I haven't stopped thinking about you, Charly. I want to be with you, now and always. Want us—you, me, Greta—to be a family."

"Really?" Her shy smile had him stroking her cheek with a finger.

"I've never wanted anything more."

And to show her how he felt, he kissed her.

This time there was no interruption. The embrace held everything in it, passion, tenderness, acceptance. It left them both trembling and aroused.

When he lay her on the bed and pressed his frame against her, she uttered a soft moan. Their lips meshed as their hands tugged and pulled at fabric, removing the clothes that separated their bodies.

There was soft laughter as he got caught in his turtleneck. An impatient huff from him as her pants button wouldn't slip through the loop. Soon enough, they were naked, their flesh touching, hands teasing.

His lips left her mouth to kiss across her jaw line then down her neck, pausing to suck at the rapid fluttering pulse.

She loved him.

He'd not expected how hearing those words made him feel.

Seen. Wanted. Protective.

Mated.

This was the woman he'd been waiting for, and it was up to him to make her happy, to give her pleasure.

His lips latched onto a nipple. She gasped and arched, uttering soft sounds of pleasure. Each utterance made him only harder.

He played with her breasts, teasing the tips, squeezing them with his hands. Such a nice handful, but there was more to explore. The scent of her arousal had him hungry.

His lips made their way down, trailing across her

rounded soft belly to nuzzle the patch of curls at her groin.

She was wet. He didn't need to look to know it. He could smell her honey. Practically taste it.

A nudge parted her thighs, and he nestled between, seeing the pink perfection of her sex, which glistened. He blew hotly on her nether lips, making her squirm. He then teased apart her sex with his fingers before he gave it a kiss.

She moaned.

The sweetest sound.

He buried his face into her honeyed heaven, licking and tasting, teasing and pleasing. Every time she mewled and squirmed, his cock swelled. What he wouldn't give to feel her come on his tongue.

But tonight was for claiming. For making her his mate not just in words but in actions. They'd had sex before, but it was different. They'd both had secrets. Both held back.

Not anymore.

He slid up the length of her body, dropping kisses along the way. When he held himself poised over her, her eyes opened, barely, the lids heavy with desire. Her swollen lips parted to whisper, "I love you, Ares."

"Oh, Charly. I love you so fucking much." He kissed her as the head of his cock penetrated. Her sex provided a warm and wet haven for him to bury himself. He went slow, but deep, seating himself fully inside and grinding. She gasped as he swirled his hips, applying pressure with his cock against her sweet spot, their bodies a perfect fit.

Her sex clenched tight around his shaft, but he could still thrust. He pumped into her, but not too fast; he wanted her to come before he did. Wanted to see her face as she climaxed.

That was the plan, but between her flesh squeezing him, her soft sounds of pleasure, and his own need, he got close to the brink. Held on, though, until she convulsed, her pussy undulating and giving him the signal to come.

And he came.

Without a condom.

Shit. He'd never forgotten one before.

She must have caught sight of his face because she whispered, "What's wrong?"

"I forgot to put on a rubber."

Her lips curved. "It will be fine. I always wanted a few kids."

"I never thought I did until you," he admitted.

"And now?"

"Now I want the whole domestic shebang."

She laughed. "Gonna keep me barefoot and pregnant?"

"Only if that's what you want. I just want to wake up every morning to your smile."

"I think that can be arranged so long as you promise to snuggle me every night."

"That might be a possibility," he teased, even as he dragged her close so he could spoon his mate.

He had to give it to his wolf. Mate had a nice ring to it.

Told you so.

What his wolf couldn't have told him was how much he'd enjoy Charly's company. They talked, they made love, they snuggled, and eventually slept.

Morning arrived way too soon with a child bouncing on the bed. "Mama, Ares! It's Christmas!"

Indeed, it was, and he already had the best present tucked by his side.

Charly opened one eye to peek at her daughter. "Is the sun even up?"

"Yup." Greta flipped off the bed and ran to open the curtain, blinding them with light.

"Did you brush your teeth and pee?" she asked next.

Greta rolled her eyes. "Yes. Can we go downstairs?"

"I still need to brush mine and tinkle," Charly stated, making Greta groan.

"Hurry, Mama. I peeked down the stairs, and Santa brought presents. Lots of them!" she exclaimed, holding her arms wide.

"Coming, munchkin. Give me a second to wake up."

Ares rolled out of bed wearing track pants and grabbed a shirt. "How about I get some coffee ready and see if there's some chocolate milk for an excited princess?"

"Yesss." Greta held out her arms, and Ares scooped her, leaving a tousled and tired-looking Charley. In her defense, they'd spent a portion of the night talking and making love rather than sleeping.

Making another pup. Wolf approved.

Very possible, seeing as how during round two Charly had shaken her head when he asked if he should go grab a condom. She'd drawn him close and whispered, "If it happens, it happens."

A baby? He couldn't think of anything more amazing.

As he entered the kitchen, no surprise; Grams was already there with freshly brewed coffee.

"Merry Christmas!" Greta exclaimed.

"And a very Merry Christmas to you too. Does someone need some fresh chocolate milk?"

"Me." Greta squirmed, and he put her down so she could run for a hug. Grams was a totally different person when around a child. She smiled, and it wasn't the terrifying grin he'd seen her use when sniping mercenaries.

"Where's Gramps?" Ares asked as he poured two mugs of coffee.

"Checking on the animals. Derek and Athena aren't up yet, but I don't imagine they'll be abed much longer." Grams pulled a glass out while Greta carefully carried the pitcher of chocolate milk to the counter.

"Charly will be down in a few minutes." A glance outside had him murmuring, "Storm's passed over."

"Yup, but the clean-up is going to take a while. The roads are sh—" Grams caught herself and said, "Slippery."

He bit back a smile as she tried to not curse in front of Greta. "I should give my mom and Selene a shout. They actually got power back last night but said the road hadn't been plowed and was about a foot deep."

"We got walloped," Grams stated, "but we'll be nice and cozy, right, sweetling?"

"We should make more cookies," Greta stated.

"I think you're right."

Grams settled Greta at the table with her chocolate milk, along with some apple slices, before sidling close to murmur, "Since I don't have a granddaughter for you to date, I approve of your choice. Charlotte's a good woman and a fine mother. She took the news of her child's lycanthropy surprisingly well."

"A good thing because we might see a repeat tonight," which reminded him... He sat beside Greta and said, "So remember how you turned into a wolf yesterday?"

She nodded.

"It's not something you can tell anybody about."

"A secret?"

He nodded.

"Mama says I shouldn't lie."

"This isn't a lie exactly, more like not telling people who wouldn't understand and might hurt us. Not everyone likes wolves."

"I like them."

"Me too. But some folks don't, which is why we have to keep that part of ourselves a secret."

Greta paused with an apple slice partway to her mouth before saying, "I don't have to keep it secret with you."

"No. Me, Athena, Selene, we all know what it means to lycan. Which is the fancy name for our wolf side. You can also trust Grams, Gramps, Derek, and Athena's mom."

"Okay." Greta agreed easily before sighing. "Mama is taking so long."

A few minutes on Christmas morning, an eternity for a child.

Soon they were in the living room, and the paper shredding began. Greta was over the moon with her fancy Barbie. Charly eyed her brand-new mix-and-match office attire with surprise.

"How did you find the time to do this?" she asked Ares.

"Athena helped," he admitted. "Thought you might like some fancy duds for the new job."

"I didn't have a chance to get you anything." Her lips turned down.

"You are the best gift ever," he said, leaning over for a kiss.

About midmorning, Greta stacked a plate with some fruitcake and peanuts from the buffet of snacks Grams laid out. As she headed for the front door, Charly asked, "Where are you going, munchkin?"

"To feed Mr. Squirrel." She pointed to the window, where a furry face with a white tuft on its head peeked in.

Ares grumbled. "I can't believe Skippy was hiding in the tree."

"A good thing. Without him, Barry might have left with Greta."

"Does this mean I can't eat him?" he groused.

"You'd better not," Charly huffed.

"Fine." He leaned close enough for her ears only and whispered, "Can I eat you then?"

The blush was so worth it.

Midafternoon got busy, as Selene arrived with his mom, bearing even more gifts. The body from the day before had been handled and the bloody snow in front of the house had been shoveled so no sign of the attack remained.

Their late afternoon dinner proved to be loud and chaotic. In other words, awesome. Ares and his small family had suddenly more than doubled in size. There was an epic turkey, farm-raised of course. Honey-glazed carrots. Mashed potatoes roasted to give them a crispy crust. Fresh buns from the oven. A stuffing to die for. Cherry pie and eclairs.

It led to much unbuttoning and unbuckling as people eased the waistband of their pants.

It was Selene who glanced at the clock and said, "It's almost time."

Greta perked at her words. "Am I going to wolf out?"

Ares and his sisters had taken turns talking to her about lycanthropy, what it meant, what to expect, what she could and couldn't do. Greta took it in, as did Charly, a mom determined to accept and support.

"Let's go find out." Selene held out her hand, and Greta took it. Charly tensed, so Ares hugged her and whispered, "Don't worry. We'll keep her safe."

"I know you will. Be careful."

"Always."

Just before the moon rose, they switched into robes. Well, the adults did. Greta wore one of Derek's plaid shirts, buttons undone. They went out onto the porch and, as the moon rose, shed their clothing. Their nude bodies shivered until the moonlight kissed their skin and they changed from flesh to fur.

Even Greta.

Off they ran, three large wolves and a little puppy, racing through the snow. Chasing each other. Yipping. Playing.

We are pack.

Beatrice put an arm around Charlotte. "I know it's hard, but I promise being a wolf mom is a special gift," she murmured. "Although, if you have a boy, be prepared for him to pee on everything."

"I heard what happened to your husband." Ares' father had been shot by a hunter.

"He knew better than to be running around in fur during hunting season. We own a large property for a reason, but for some reason, that night, he went elsewhere."

Charlotte wouldn't let Greta make that mistake.

She stood watching as the wolves barked and raced in the snow, but all too soon, they headed into the forest, a safe section according to Gramps.

Despite planning to stay up until they returned, Charlotte fell asleep on the couch and woke to cold hands on her cheeks.

"Mama!"

"Munchkin." Charlotte roused immediately. "How was it?"

Greta grinned. "I howled at the moon."

"You had fun?"

"The best. But it's not fair."

"What isn't?"

Greta's lips turned down. "Girls can't pee on trees."

To which Ares, who entered the living room

wearing a robe, laughed. "How about I pee on them for you?"

And that was how her day ended. In a relationship with a werewolf, the mother of a puppy, crazy happy, and in love.

Best Christmas ever.

EPILOGUE

Greta carefully balanced the tray as she entered the bedroom. Grandma Bee—because she was the honey-bee lady—had helped her prepare the special breakfast and then carried it up the stairs. But Greta wanted to be the one to present it.

She wobbled only slightly as she brought it to the bed holding her mama and Ares.

Mama's eyes popped open, and she smiled. "Morning, munchkin."

"Happy Valentine's Day," Greta announced as she held up the tray. It wobbled and almost tilted over.

Ares bounced out of bed, no shirt but pants on. He and Mama always wore pajamas, not like the first time she found them naked in bed.

"Let me help you, princess." He set the tray on Mama's lap before turning to grab her in a big hug.

"Happy Valentine's Day to my special lady," he murmured, nuzzling his nose against hers.

She giggled. "I'm a little girl, not a lady."

"Actually, you're my princess, and as the special royal in my life, I got you a present."

"Oooh." She couldn't help but coo in delight.

"Sit beside your mom while I grab it."

Mama snuggled Greta into her side as she chewed on some bacon. Ares returned with two boxes, a little one for mama, a large one for her.

Greta smirked at her mom. "Mine's bigger."

Mama snorted. "I noticed."

Ares scooted into bed, keeping her tucked between him and Mama as he said, "Open them."

"You first, munchkin."

The first thing Greta saw beyond the pink tissue paper? A stuffed wolf wearing a pink bow. She hugged it. "My very own puppy."

"There's more," he nudged, pointing to an envelope at the bottom.

She opened it and saw a paper with lots of words. "Is it a story?"

"Kind of. It's the tale of a man who met a woman and her lovely princess daughter one day and fell in love. Loved them so much he wanted them to be with him forever. And so he adopted the little princess."

"Adopted," Greta repeated the word, and a smile pulled her lips because she knew what it meant. Mama had talked to her about it. "Does this make you my dada?"

"It does. I hope it's okay."

"Yesss!" Greta flung herself at him and hugged him so tight he choked and begged, "Mercy."

She giggled. Ares was always so funny. She plopped back in between her mama and her new dada. She'd just gotten the bestest present. Poor mama with her little box. "Mama's turn."

Mama's eyes got watery as she opened her gift. Inside was a ring.

Dada sounded as if he were choking when he said, "Charly, I love you more than anything. Will you marry me?"

"Say yes, Mama. Then he'll really be my dada."

"That paper already says he is, but I guess we can make it official."

They kissed. Gross. But Greta was okay with it because that's what mamas and dadas did when they loved each other.

The presents weren't done though. Mama had one too, an envelope with Greta and Ares written on it.

She didn't understand the weird picture, black with swirly gray and white, but Ares did. He leaned down and whispered, "You're going to be a big sister."

"I am!" Best Valentine's Day ever.

MY BOYFRIEND MARKS TREES

Selene was finally going on her cruise. Minus her mother. Not her choice, but apparently, as a new grandma, her mom had a duty to spoil. Selene argued an aunt had the same right. However, her family insisted she go and booked her into a singles voyage that coincided with Valentine's Day.

As if she needed help getting laid. Men hit on her all the time, but none kept her attention. Selene wanted a grand love affair. Wanted to be swept off her feet like Athena with Derek and Charlotte with her brother.

Was it so much to ask for?

Mom kept saying one day she'd meet the one and she'd know. She sure hoped so because she was beginning to feel like a third wheel every time she hung out with her siblings.

The plane to Orlando took just under four hours. Then there was the bus the cruise provided that brought them to port, where most of the passengers were her mom's age.

This could get interesting.

Especially since the one elderly couple had pineapples plastered all over their luggage. When they smiled at her and asked if she'd like to join them for a drink, she politely declined. Was this going to be a cruise for older swingers?

Yikes.

Maybe she'd just stay in her room with a book and order in food.

As the line to board shuffled along, the embarkation delayed until six thirty at night, she noticed the large dogs sniffing people. Drug dogs. She didn't have any drugs, but given her lycan heritage, she wasn't surprised they barked in her direction.

As a woman wearing latex gloves and a uniform waved at her to step aside, Selene resigned herself to being strip-searched and questioned.

To her surprise, a deep voice with a slight accent said, "That won't be necessary. She's with me."

She glanced in surprise at the handsome man in the slick suit. "I'm sorry. Do I know you?"

"No, but I plan to rectify that once we're on board," said with a smile and a wink.

A shiver went through her.

Maybe she would have fun after all.

GET READY BECAUSE SELENE'S ABOUT TO MEET HER LOVE MATCH IN THE NEXT BOOK, MY BOYFRIEND BITES.

www.ingramcontent.com/pod-product-compliance
Lightning Source LLC
LaVergne TN
LVHW031540060526
838200LV00056B/4584